BLACK MAGE CURSED

CLEAVE BOURBON

Black Mage Cursed

Copyright © 2024 by Cleave Bourbon

All rights reserved.

No part of this book may be reproduced in any form or by any electronic or mechanical means, including information storage and retrieval systems, without written permission from the author, except for the use of brief quotations in a book review.

This is a work of fiction. Names, characters, businesses, places, events, and incidents are either the product of the author's imagination or are used fictitiously. Any resemblance to actual persons, living or dead, events, or locals is entirely coincidental

Contact info: cleavebourbon@cleavebourbon.com

Front Cover Design by Shadesilver Publishing

Print Cover Design by Shadesilver Publishing

Editor: Courtney Umphress www.courtneyumphress.com

SECOND EDITION : August 2024

10 9 8 7 6 5 4 3 2

Join in on the fun!

Cleave Bourbon's Fantasy News

My newsletter has free books, sales on books, exclusive deals, and more. You can also get the latest news on my new releases! Just scan the QR code below.

BLACK MAGE CURSED
THE MAGE OF NECROMANCY
CLEAVE BOURBON

SHADESILVER PUBLISHING

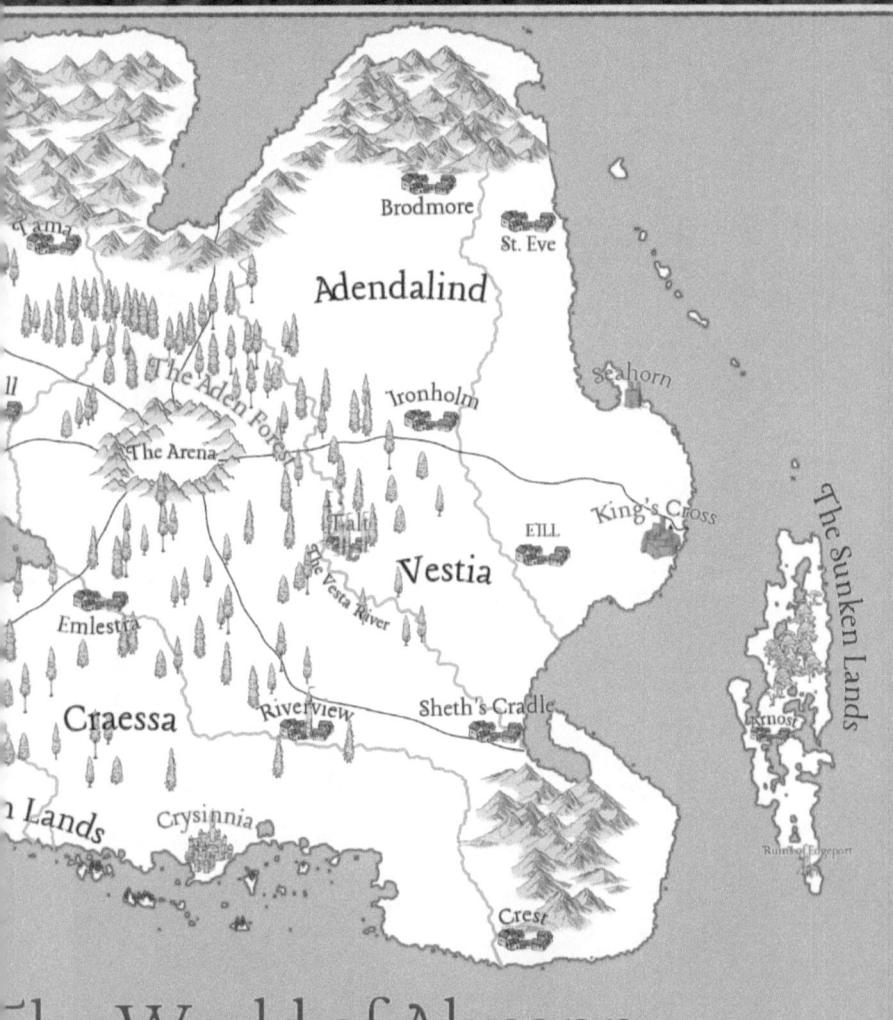

CONTENTS

1. Prologue — 1
2. Caught — 4
3. Adversary — 8
4. Sacrifice — 19
5. The River's Edge — 26
6. The Meeting — 31
7. Tanyth Veridian — 39
8. The City — 46
9. Clever Secrets — 56
10. Dark Mistress — 63
11. A Tale of Winter's Chill — 71
12. The Young Man in the Market — 78
13. Before Dawn — 85
14. Reunion — 90
15. Daggers of the Soul — 98
16. The Broken Lands — 105
17. Cracks in the Marble — 115
18. Danse Macabre — 121

19.	Memorial	128
20.	A Grave Mistake	134
21.	Black Mage	141
22.	The Way is East	148
23.	The Sunken Lands	155
24.	Abominations	160
25.	Life and Death	167
26.	White Mage	172
27.	The Last Stand	177
28.	Futility	184
29.	The Bramble Path	190
Also By Cleave Bourbon		195
Glossary		196

Prologue
From Red to Black

Excerpt from Red Mage–

"How did you even know I was the Red Mage all those years ago?"

Sarren smiled wickedly, "You don't recognize me. I didn't think you did, but I wasn't certain until now. It's the doom of the noble class. They never bother to look into the face of their servants. You never bothered to look at me."

"What are you talking about?"

"I was your mother's handmaiden. I watched you. I set up your meeting with Tovo. It was me! I did it all! I followed you to the city of Talt and to the Sephera family."

"That's why you disguised yourself as a man." She looked at Thessa, "You have failed Sarren, you can't turn my own blood against me."

"I never do anything I haven't meticulously planned out. You should know that by now!" She lurched forward and stabbed her twisted dagger into Hana's stomach. "I may not be able to kill you, but I can have another do it." Hana fell to her knees. "Get the dagger from the girl." Sarren commanded.

Hana looked back to see Thessa dive for the dagger as a young man beat her to it. Thessa grabbed the boy by the waist.

"Let him go, child," Sarren said. Thessa began to change again, and it freed the boy from her. Hana crawled toward Sarren, but she easily sidestepped her.

"Kill the Red Mage!"

The boy stabbed Hana in the back repeatedly. Hana felt no pain, and it was then she remembered the dagger was her own. It was the ruby-handled dagger of the Red Mage; it wouldn't hurt her. Thessa ran up behind the boy and attacked him in the throat.

"No, Thessa, that's my dagger!" Hana pleaded.

Sarren screeched with glee until she realized what Hana was saying. Thessa now had the dagger, and she was inches away.

"No, Thessa, that dagger can't hurt me! Don't do it! Just drop it!"

It was too late, Thessa plunged Hana's dagger into the heart of Sarren. The blade of the Red Mage, which had no effect on Hana, was deadly to Sarren. Hana watched in horror as the life force drained from Sarren and entered Thessa. A black fog rolled out from Sarren's body as she fell with Thessa still gripping the dagger. Thessa looked at her mother with terror. Her eyes turned red and her facial features contorted while she collapsed onto Sarren. Hana went to her, still holding the wound in her stomach. She took the blood from her wound and began smearing it on the now unconscious Thessa.

"I can turn you back." Her tears flowed, blocking her vision. "Please, I can turn you back!" The blood burned Thessa's skin rather than helping her. Thessa began to whimper, and Hana wiped the blood from her. "I'm sorry, I'm sorry." She took the Well of Life stone from her pocket and rubbed it over her wound. The green light from the stone healed her. She tried to use it on Thessa, but it too burned her skin. She moved away from her daughter and Hana's eyes caught sight of Tovo, who was still standing near the throne. He gazed forward with a catatonic expression.

Chapter 1
Caught

Ephaltus took a deep breath and entered the Ocularius Magnus room located on the upper floor of the Earth Chamber. He often used this smaller oculus when he needed a bit of privacy or if he just wanted to do a quick check on one of the mages without having to go to the arsenal and fire up the bigger, more cumbersome machine. They both worked the same way and logged the time spent on them as if they were one machine, so it didn't matter which one was used at any given time. The only thing that sometimes gave the machine an issue was when both were being used at the same time. The double use made it difficult for the machine to keep and accurate account of the time used and Ephaltus was adamant with keeping the oculus records correctly to maintain calibration times and prevent cheating by the gods and their agents.

He sat in the chair situated in front of the lens and dialed the out ring until the internal circles focused on black. He was worried about the new Black Mage and how she might be reacting to her new role. Marlee had talked him into sending her mother, the Red Mage and Asleth with her, away from the chamber where she became the Black Mage. The oculus whirred and crackled as it spun to life and focused on a random black cat. Confused, Ephaltus restarted the lens, and it focused on Thessa, the new mage stood alone in the chamber. It appeared she was using her magic on the corpse of the former Black Mage. Concerned, he leaned in closer to get a better view. It was then he noticed an eyeball in the corner of the great lens. It retreated as soon as he glimpsed it.

"Oh, no you don't, cheater!" Ephaltus exclaimed as he chased the eye by turning the lens furiously in the direction it had retreated. He caught a glimpse of it again and turned it further. "I'll have some strong words with that apprentice of mine the next time I see her for not calibrating this thing again like I have told her a million times to do." The lens landed on the Red Mage. He stopped for a moment. Even though he couldn't hear her, it appeared as if she was crying and screaming at Asleth, the Grey Mage. He turned up the volume.

"We have to go back. Why did you do that?" She was saying.

Asleth was shaking his head. "It wasn't me. Here I will try to get us back there."

Ephaltus saw the eye and turned the lens again chasing after it. He caught it when the lens focused on a candle with an unusually bright flame. Behind the candle stood a man with dark blond, almost brown hair, dressed in a dark mustard robe manipulating the flame. He glanced at the circles around the lens to see the eye had led him to the possible future viewing lens. He magically captured the spying eye and expelled it. He recognized the chamber behind the agent. It was one used by Cassany. "What arrogance to use one of her own chambers to cheat. Surely, she would have known if she got caught, I would know exactly who was doing the cheating. She probably doesn't even care. He spun the lens to calibration position and began turning all the knobs and circles to zero position. "Well, we'll stop this spying nonsense right now. It was a chore to turn all the knobs, lenses and circles back to zero and turn the machine off and on. That's the reason, he wagered, his apprentice didn't like to do it and often acted as if she merely forgot about it. Calibration took about half an hours all total, but it was worth it to keep the prying eyes from looking in on their rivels.

"Calibrating?" Marlee said as she entered the room.

Ephaltus gave her a derisive grunt. "Something you seem to forget to do far too often. I have been telling you for weeks not to forget but here I am, recalibrating for you...again."

"Sorry."

"No, no don't apologize. Don't even begin. You say the words, but they have no meaning if you don't at least strive to do better. Saying sorry just gives you a way out of trouble and then it's quickly forgotten while you just do it again. Saying you're sorry gets me off your back, but your mistake will return time and again and then will once again be dismissed as easily as the last sorry upon your lips. No, this time it will be a punishment. You must learn from your mistakes and reminding you with just a simple please isn't working. It needs to be more substantial this time. No more warnings."

"What did you have in mind?"

"I don't know yet, but it will have to be something that you will not soon forget."

"What happened. What did you see?"

"Oh, someone from Cassany was spying on the Red Mage. No telling how long this spy was watching. Cassany is one of the worst good for cheating. The next time I see one of them cheating, I am going to call a meeting of the gods and remind them the rules of the tournament now that their champions are emerging."

"That might be a good idea." Marlee agreed. "But why call a meeting next time? Whynot now?"

"I'll give them one more chance. We are still early in our preparations. There is nota lot to be gained from their spying quite yet. Besides, I have better things to do."

"Like what?"

"Don't be daft. Like watching the new Black Mage. She was doing something – unusual earlier. She was fiddling with the dead body of the former Black Mage. As soon as the lens is cleared and recalibrated, I think we need to see exactly what she was doing."

Marlee jumped in and began to turn some of the knobs and lens to zero. "This will go faster if I help."

"First smart thing I have heard you say in a while."

Chapter 2
Adversary

Thessa stood in disbelief as Asleth shrouded Hana with his cloak and they both disappeared from the cavern. Hana had abandoned her. She scoffed at the corpse of Sarren, whose face was hidden just beneath the cloudy water. She felt a little sick because of her next thought, but she was not about to be left alone, and she was confident Tovo would make a poor companion in his present state.

"Oh, no, you don't." The tears came uncontrollably, and she wiped them away angrily as if she were mad at them for flowing. She focused once again on the corpse of Sarren. "I can't let you getaway with the horrible things you have done! I can't let you die so easily without paying for the things you have done to people and what you have done tome!" She reached out to Sarren and let some of the energy she still felt pulsing through her body enter the former Black Mage. With a jolt which also startled Thessa, Sarren abruptly sat up out of the water. The woman immediately felt around for the dagger wound, but it was no longer there. Her eyes were full of anger when her gaze met Thessa's, "Fool! What have you done?" She pushed herself up from the pallid water and tried in vain to attack Thessa, but her legs gave way, and she stumbled. Thessa stepped out of Sarren's way and let her fall to her hands and knees.

"You are bound to me now, Sarren. I am your master." She didn't know where the words came from, but she believed them as they reverberated inside her head. She knew as her energy changed within her that the words were exact.

"I... I won't let you," She began to search around the milky water splashing back and forth.

Thessa lifted her hand, and the ruby-handled dagger appeared. Sarren stopped splashing when she saw the dagger. She lurched toward Thessa with determination and took the dagger from Thessa's hand before she knew what was happening and plunged the blade into her own chest. It did nothing. Shocked, she looked at Thessa and then plunged it into her repeatedly, but nothing happened. Frustrated, she threw the dagger into the water. Thessa opened her hand, and the dagger reappeared. She tucked it inside her belt.

"What... I mean, why did you bring me back?"

Thessa met her gaze. "Because it was a mistake for you to die. I made a mistake. You need to live to regret what you have done."

Sarren laughed. "I regret nothing!"

"You think this is all a joke?" Thessa asked.

"Yes, and I think it's funny. You have no idea the curse you have brought upon yourself. You think, no, you believe I had free will! Do you believe that I willingly flitted around at my behest? The goddess ruling the Black Mage is ruthless. If you take up the mantle, you will do as I did, possibly even worse. You can't wipe your hands clean from it. You are the Black Mage now. You freed me from it." She clenched her fists, "I was freed from it. I would rather be forced to serve you than to serve Cassany. Your goddess will demand you make horrible sacrifices in her name. Even while serving you, I am free from it. I am free of her at long last."

"I feel no sympathy for you. You will serve me and help me get rid of this."

Sarren's face went somber, "Oh, you poor girl. You don't understand. I may not have a choice whether to serve you, but I can take comfort in knowing you will serve her! You will never get rid of this curse barring your death. As long as you serve her, she will make sure no one harms you."

"I killed you!"

"I failed her once too often, or maybe she saw more power in you. I can't know the goddess' reasoning, but I think maybe she let you kill me."

"I don't want to be the Black Mage! Take it back!"

"Tsk, Tsk, too bad, isn't it? You can try to fight it until one day you realize the futility of it, and then, slowly, you will give in to it as I once did. Do you think I began my journey as a ruthless, heartless woman?"

"We'll see about that. I'll find a way to get out of this."

Sarren grinned, "Oh, what's your plan? We travel around looking for someone to kill you and take your place? You can't stay among the living and transfer the mantle of the Black Mage to somebody else; you know. Someone must kill you, and as I stated, the goddess must have chosen you for a reason." She carefully righted herself onto her wobbly legs." I can't wait to see how you handle the sacrifices."

"You mentioned sacrifices before. What sacrifices?"

"You will feel the terrible pull and urge soon enough. It will happen innocently at first. Something small will set you off and then you will be on your way. Cassany will demand blood. She hates the creations of her siblings and seeks to twist and pervert them. It's the reason you can raise dead to do your bidding. She also wants her servant, you, to kill them. Of course, not so many as to alert the other gods, but at least one per day, or two every other day."

"I don't believe you. You are trying to rattle me."

"She will play mind games with you and torture you, especially if you fight her will."

"I won't do it! I hated killing when I hungered as a blood feeder, and I will not kill for the goddess."

"You will. The urge is too strong."

"I will create a couple of blood feeders as you made me, and I will let them kill for food."

Sarren shook her head. "That won't work. Your blood feeders kill separately. You will be demanded to make a sacrifice in addition to those your blood feeders kill. Besides, killing is killing whether you do it or have your minions do it, your hands will be just as stained with blood."

"You're lying!"

"No."

"If it is demanded of me, I will make you do it."

"No, it will not count. She will demand you do it by your own hand."

"I won't!"

"This is pointless," Sarren said. "I have told you what you need to know. Release me!"

"I will never release you," Thessa said in almost a whisper. "You will suffer alongside me."

"No, I will not let you." She raised a dagger and Thessa recognized it as the Red Mage dagger. She felt for the dagger inside her belt, but the dagger disappeared.

"How did you steal that from me?"

Sarren plunged the dagger into her own chest and then twisted horribly, much more forcibly than before. This time the dagger dug in and Sarren fell to her death once more.

Thessa took the ruby handled dagger and willed it to disappear. It popped out of her hand and was gone. She then reached down and resurrected Sarren again. The former Black Mage writhed and kicked as she came back from the realm of the dead. The woman looked around horrified, "What have you done to me? This is impossible! You can't raise me twice. I couldn't even do that."

"I need your help. You used to be the Black Mage. You will now teach me."

"How? How did you bring me back a second time?"

"Do it again and I will just bring you back a third time. You cannot escape me. I need your knowledge."

The resurrected woman laughed, and her eyes went wild, "You simple fool. Where has your mommy gone? If she were here, she might tell you never to do something as foolish as you have just done."

"You *will* curb your madness! My mother and I will cross paths again." Thessa realized the second resurrection might have done something to Sarren's sanity. She was confused and acted out irrationally.

"What have you done to me?" Sarren repeated, and Thessa began to pity her a bit.

The resurrected woman stumbled back looking down and searching her clothing for something, "Ah, there you are." She grinned and produced another dagger. Thessa feared she might use it, so she took a step back until Sarren began to laugh again, "This dagger is the onyx-handled dagger of the Black Mage, useless on you now, I suppose." She looked around their feet, "Where is that red dagger?"

"You will instruct me. You're dead. I control you now. Isn't that how this is supposed to work?"

The resurrected woman stepped closer," Until I kill you and regain my power. You idiot, you don't resurrect the former Black Mage." She grabbed the Thessa by the throat. "All I have to do is cut your throat."

"You've lost your mind," she gasped, "You just said that dagger would not harm me."

The Black Mage pushed Thessa away, and she fell forcibly onto the waterlogged floor, one leg slipping in the feted water. Thessa regained her composure and was forceful again, "I am your master now. I can stop you from your nasty intentions."

"All I have to do is wait. You can't watch me all the time. I will find a way to kill you."

"I may have the solution to that," A woman in white said as she walked in from the entrance. A startled Sarren threw the dagger she held at the woman in full force.

The woman in white screeched like a psychotic bird, and the blade deflected off the sound and fell into the dirty water. She continued to move toward them, "All you have to do is cut off her arms."

"What did you just say?" Thessa asked.

"She can't stab you to death or slit your throat without her arms, cut them off."

"Who in the two hells are you?" Sarren asked.

"I am Fia, the White Mage. I would have thought that obvious because, well, I'm wearing white, and I just screamed your dagger away."

"Oh, yes, because all the mages wear clothes of their color." Sarren sneered.

"Someone doesn't have a sense of humor." Fia said. "Pity."

"There is no need to cut off her arms. I know she can't kill me. I resurrected her. I am her master now. All this posturing is to frighten me, but I know the truth. She is having a little trouble adapting is all."

"Cut off her head, then. She doesn't need it and it will shut her up." Fia said.

Sarren was appalled, "Removal of the head will permanently kill the resurrected. It's one sure way to do it."

"Shut up, Sarren," Thessa commanded." She is trying to get to you like you were trying to get to me."

"That's not true at all," Fia said. "I don't think it is, anyway."

"I can't cut off any of her body parts," Thessa said. "The truth of the matter is Sarren is dead, and I know I have complete control over her. She must obey me. She can't kill me."

"Uh, no, she will try to find a way to kill you and turn back into the Black Mage herself."

"She can't. You know nothing of how the Black Mage's powers work." Thessa realized as the essence of the Black Mage passed to her, she had gained some knowledge with it. Cassany must have made it so the new mage would have an advantage, or all the mages have a collective memory.

"Maybe not. But I would love to try it and find out."

"Try what, cutting off her arms or tryout the Black Mage powers?"

"Yes, to both."

"You are evil." The Black Mage said." Look at you with your beauty and blonde hair, you even wear white, and you are called the White Mage, but it's clear you are a bad person."

"I don't see what my color, beauty, or manner of dress has to do with my demeanor. Does your black hair and gaunt appearance make you evil? If you want to keep this woman, Sarren is it? And you want her to train you then you must do some pretty unspeakable things because she will definitely not hesitate to do whatever she has to do to take your life. You do realize you will never be able to reform her. She is as she is forever."

"I never wanted to be the Black Mage. I should let her kill me and take it all back."

"You know, this gives me a great idea. I need your help." She turned to Sarren, "But first, let me help you. I'll cut her arms off."

"Wait, leave her arms intact. what do you need my help with?"

"The Blue Mage is our ally, yours and mine. I need you to help me with rescuing him. I need your magic to do it." She looked at the man standing next to the throne. 'I'm sorry, I must know. Who is that man, and what in the two hells is he supposed to be doing? "He's just standing there staring."

"He's my father, Tovo. Sarren used him and killed him when she was the Black Mage."

"How did she use him?" Fia asked.

"She used him to trick my mother, and then she killed him."

"Your mother did?"

"No, Sarren did. It was part of her plan, her strategy, against the Red Mage." Thessa knew the White Mage was just asking questions to ask them. She already knew who killed Tovo. She just wanted Thessa to say it for some reason.

Fia's jaw dropped, "And you don't want to cut off her arms?" She walked over to Sarren and stood behind her. She began to hum a beautiful melodic tune into her ear.

"What are you doing?" Thessa asked.

"Hold her still," Fia instructed.

"She isn't going anywhere," Thessa said.

Fia's tune became a song. As she sang, bands of light surrounded Sarren, binding her, and then they disappeared." There, she can't move except for her legs. She can come along with us, but she is paralyzed from the waist up."

"You wench!" Sarren said.

"Careful, or I will paralyze your ugly face too!" Fia said, pointing a perfectly manicured finger at her. "This will give you time to decide what to do with her."

"Thank you," Thessa said. "But it's not necessary. She is not a threat to me at all." She looked down at the ground where she had rescued her mother.

"What is it?" Fia asked.

"What did you do with my mother, Sarren?" Thessa asked. "Why did she leave like that?"

"Nothing, I was too busy dying, remember."

Fia put her hand on Thessa's shoulder," I'm sure there is a good explanation for her leaving. Why didn't you resurrect your father?"

Thessa shrugged, "Why don't you mind your own business?" She was deciding whether she even liked this White Mage.

"Don't get testy, I was just wondering."

"You'll know when I get testy." Thessa said. "You ask a lot of questions. I don't think I'll answer them."

Fia eyed her for a moment, "Well, Thessa, if you don't mind. I'm not certain about how much time we have. We had better get going. I will explain what happened, where the Blue Mage is, and what I need you to do while we travel. I have a boat we can use to go back upriver."

"We don't need a boat," Sarren said." The Black Mage has another way to travel over distances."

"Now, see," Fia summoned the dagger Sarren tried to throw at her from the dirty water with a whistle. She held it up, looking at the mud-tarnished blade, "That wasn't so difficult, was it. You are already proving your worth."

Thessa summoned the power from the dead around them and channeled it into the travel spell. She knew it instinctively. Just before the spell went off in a spectacular whoosh of air, Thessa made eye contact with Sarren, who was smiling devilishly. A terrible feeling washed over her, but it was too late. The two women before her faded out into the rushing air before her eyes. Fia, Sarren, and Thessa left the chamber, and all the fires burned out immediately. The empty corpse of Tovo collapsed headfirst into the feted water.

***

After she exited the Black Mage's portal, Fia bent over and wretched. Sarren chuckled.

"You could have warned me." Fia protested.

Sarren chuckled again. "Where's the fun in that? I thought you had traveled by her spell before."

Thessa took in their surroundings. They were still in the desert with a city a ways ahead in the distance. "Where are we? Sarren, if you deceived me on how I was supposed to use that portal, I'll let Fia cut off your arms and feed them to you."

"I told you correctly. The Blue Mage must be nearby."

"I'm going to perform a directional dance. I suggest you both keep your eyes focused on the other direction while I do so. The dance has another purpose that tends to blind those who see it or worse." Fia said.

"You forget. I am already dead. Your dance will not hurt me." Sarren said.

"Do what you want, but when you're blind, don't complain."

"I'll make sure she doesn't look." Thessa assured her.

Fia performed the dance and had her arrow again, this time for the location of the Blue Mage. It did indeed point to the city. "Hmm, Zedy was right after all. He did escape on his own. I'll meet up with the boys and meet you outside of Emlestra in a day or so for the illusion to get rid of Danton like I told you."

"I am not really comfortable about bringing someone back from the realm of the dead, Fia."

Fia put her hand on Thessa's shoulder. "It will be an easy thing for you and your new powers. Trust me. Arran and I have it all planned out. You will just need to get there before he is too far gone. I will send a song on the breeze to summon you."

Thessa nodded. Fia smiled at her and left following her spell toward the location of the Blue Mage.

"What now?" Thessa asked as she looked to Sarren for some kind of answer.

"Why are you looking at me? I have no idea what to do."

"I think I need to find my mother and Asleth and find out why they left me there."

Fia nodded, "That might be a good idea, I wish you the best. Thank you. I will send the summons song when I am ready for you. I will be seeing you soon."

Thessa nodded and took hold of Sarren. "Come on Sarren. Mother will know what to do with you." She initiated the portal and the two disappeared into the black portal cloud.

Chapter 3
Sacrifice

Thessa felt a pull on her body. She felt Sarren traveling with her rip from her spell and disappear. There was a crack like that of lightning in a spring thunderstorm, a lurch, and then she found herself in a clearing surrounded by tall, unfamiliar trees. She looked around for Sarren, but she was nowhere to be seen. A slow panic began to rise from the depths of her soul. She took several steps toward the nearest grouping of trees, then stopped. She whirled around and took a few steps toward the trees on the opposite side before falling on her weakened knees. The spell had taken a toll. She lifted her eyes at the sound of a rumbling coming from the center of the clearing. The rumbling became louder, and the ground began to vibrate, and then the grass and dirt formed into the figure of a human. Clods of dirt fell away, dried, and blew into the air with strong gusts of wind.

Grass molded into strands of hair that fell to the figure's back. A dirt-clumped face took on definition, and two red eyes protruded for a moment out of the head. The face turned a beautiful shade of brown and the red eyes also turned a rich coco brown. The rest of the dirt fell away, revealing a flowing white gown. On top of the clearly female form's head appeared a crown of gold. A set of ugly black wings formed out of the woman's back. The figure stood about two heads taller than Thessa. She sauntered almost glided toward her with wings flapping. Thessa knew right after she formed who the woman was. She was Cassany, the winged goddess of death and the underworld, presumably in one of her many guises.

Thessa, already on her knees, just awkwardly bowed her head. She did not want to provoke the goddess until she could find a way to get away from her grasp. Cassany raised her hand to the side and Sarren appeared out of thin air. The former Black Mage fell to her knees and bowed with her arms outstretched.

"My goddess," she said. Cassany just glared at her silently. "Please, goddess. Let me explain."

Cassany raised her hand and Sarren began to disintegrate. The woman screamed in agony as parts of her disappeared in a brown dust and fell to the ground with a swooshing sound. Cassany was punishing Sarren for the sheer pleasure of it. The goddess turned her gaze to Thessa. Strangely, Thessa was unafraid. Something inside her head reminded her the goddess could not harm her. She was the Black Mage now.

"I wish you had not done that. I needed her. I would appreciate it if you would bring her back." Thessa said defiantly.

Cassany's eyes narrowed, "You dare demand favors from me?" she said in a low rumbling voice.

"I do, goddess. You would do well to bring her back if you want me strong enough to defeat my mother and the others in the tournament."

"Ah, your mother. So, you say you will fight her willingly?"

"Yes, goddess. If you allow me to have Sarren as my teacher."

"Pitiful! Your mother has not abandoned you." Cassany said with contempt. "You humans are so quick to jump to conclusions, the wrong conclusions. She was taken away from you against her will by the Tourney Master and his naïve apprentice."

"You were there?"

"I had a spy looking on through their looking device until the Tourney Master caught her. Your mother searches for you now, as we speak. Had you not left the cavern; she would have returned to find you." Cassany said.

"Why would you tell me such a thing after I said I was willing to fight her? You are the mother of lies. It's in your nature to stir up trouble."

"Yes, I am the mother of lies, but ask yourself. What would telling you about your mother do for me? She would hunt for you, find you, and explain it to you. That oaf, the Grey Mage, will back up her story and you will forgive her. I have just cut all that nonsense away. Now you can forgive her, get all that worry and grief out of the way of your learning, so we may start building your power instead of going through all that drama."

"Fine, but I still need Sarren."

"Why? She has done nothing but betray you. She will forever betray you."

"And she must pay for all that betrayal."

"Ah, I like that," Cassany waved her arm and Sarren reappeared as an apparition. "You can command her this way. Only you may see her. It will make it easier for you to learn."

"A cat, goddess. I have always wanted a cat."

"You wish for me to give you... a cat?"

"Sarren, Sarren can be my cat. I can handle her as a cat."

"Oh no, goddess, please do not make me into a cat. I hate cats." Sarren pleaded. She investigated the face of Cassany then gasped, "I mean, I love cats."

"A cat, goddess, and you know she hates cats. It will be a perfect punishment." Thessa said.

"I shall consider your request." Cassany said.

"Also, what am I to do about Fia?" Thessa inquired. "She is asking me to do something I am uncomfortable with."

"I have no intention of interfering with another god's champion yet. The White Mage is an ally for the time being. In fact, your ally and the matter of which you speak is the reason I am here before you. You will have certain duties to perform in addition to your training. You will need to make certain sacrifices to gain power and keep my favor."

"If you mean I have to kill people like I did as a blood feeder, I won't do it!" Thessa knew the goddess needed her. She hoped she wasn't going too far.

She could see Cassany fuming at the words, but the goddess regained her composure, "Then you will like the first task I give you. It is the resurrection the White Mage wants you to perform. I want to bring the one called Danton back from my realm. I do not wish for him to die just yet, and I can't send him back directly. I need my Black Mage to do it."

"There's no trick is there? The person won't become some horrible blight on humanity or something?"

"No, of course not," she said sweetly. "He is the son of the king. It will save your allies from the king's wrath if his son returns alive rather than the way he is now."

"Why have you taken on that sickly sweet tone? You're lying."

Cassany's cheeks turned a fiery red, but she remained in control of her anger. Thessa was impressed at her fortitude. "See for yourself. Go back to your allies, the Blue Mage and the White Mage. They are already regretting killing the young prince. Resurrect him and send him home. I will do the rest. Since you do not like my tone, I am no longer asking you. I am now commanding you to resurrect him." She raised her hand and Thessa fell to the ground, pinned under an unseen force. "I know you believe you are somehow protected from my wrath but know this. There are ways for me to punish you and ultimately replace you if I need to. The tournament is still far enough away for me to train a new champion. You had better learn to watch yourself with me and learn quickly. Look to your cat for an example."

Sarren was horrified, "What? No wait." With the wave of Cassany's hand, Sarren had become a cat with all black fur.

Cassany let Thessa up and faced her. "Sarren will instruct you. You will hear her thoughts in your mind. I have little time for you now, but I will be in touch. Go to your allies and resurrect Sir Danton!" With that, Cassany flowed back into the ground, "Tell her of the gold, Sarren." She said before she was completely gone.

Sarren hissed. Thessa could hear her in her mind. *You angered her. You stupid girl.*

"Shut up cat and tell me how to get out of here?"

This is the clearing. It doesn't really have a name other than that. Cassany loves to bring her servants here to talk, maim, or kill them. She would have told you much more had you not disrespected her.

"Disrespect her?" Thessa was on the verge of shouting, "I don't know what that even means. I don't serve her."

Oh, you serve her now. You are the Black Mage. Sarren looked off into the distance, *I wonder if it was Cassany who helped you with that. It must be the case. Someone like you could never have defeated me so easily otherwise.*

"What would she have told me?"

The ins and outs of being the Black Mage. Remember when I told you how you would have to offer sacrifices? Well, you just sealed your fate with that. This resurrection may be easy for you, but you will have to do much worse later.

"I won't kill people for her."

Oh, you will. She told me to show you the gold. You are rich for a reason. You will... you know what? I am tired of trying to explain it to you. I think I will let you discover that for yourself. The only advice I will give you is you should go find a city to start off in and when you get good at disguise, you can move into smaller cities the way I did.

"Disguise?"

Yes, look at you. Your mother and becoming the Black Mage may have cured you from the beast you had inside of you, but you still look like a blood feeder. Here, pick me up. Thessa reached down and took the cat into her arms. Sarren pawed at a strand of Thessa's hair. *You can change your appearance. I chose to look like a man for the respect factor, but you can look however you want. It's part of the Black Mage's power skill set. The best infiltrator is the one no one can identify. It allows you to do the unspeakable things you are going todo for Cassany.*

"I already told you. I am not going to kill people for the pleasure of a twisted goddess."

Sarren looked at her with bewilderment, *Really, what do you plan to do then? She will not grant you free will.*

"Where is this gold then?" Thessa asked, ignoring what Sarren had said.

Did you hear me?

"Yes, I heard you. Now answer my question, please."

It's around. I will show you because the goddess commands it. We must travel to Emlestra, but first we must retrieve the coin.

"Coin?"

It's the key to finding your treasure. You can't get to it without it. We can transport to my hiding place.

"Is it far?"

Not far.

"Good, then we go by land, the old fashion way."

What? Why?

"Because you knew as soon as we left the cavern, Cassany would detect my magic and intercept me. Cassany knows that spell and uses it to track my movements, doesn't she?"

Sarren nodded.

"Then we go by foot. Cassany can find me some other way."

It won't stop her.

"Maybe it will slow her down."

She will be waiting to see if you go to the White Mage. She will seek you out if you don't go right now.

Thessa took a deep breath, "Okay, once more. How do I go directly to her?"

Concentrate on the White Mage and you will us to her.

Thessa concentrated as Sarren moved to get comfortable in Thessa's arms. In a burst of dark smoky light, Thessa used the spell.

Chapter 4
The River's Edge

Thessa could hear Fia talking, and she quickly realized the White Mage was not alone. Sarren ran up before her right under Fia's feet. "Sarren, what are you doing? Come back!"

"Where did you come from little one?" She heard Fia ask.

"She's with me." Thessa said, stepping out to where they could see her. Fia was there but so was a handsome man with dark hair and blue eyes and an old man dressed in dirty white. "Turns out I *can* use the travel spell."

"That's great!" Fia began. "It worked itself out."

Thessa saw the corpse of Danton lying before Fia and she knew she was there for him. She hoped it wasn't too late to revive him. She had to come back to revive him. "I didn't really have a choice. I was commanded to come here and bring him back from the dead."

"Commanded?" Fia asked. " I only asked you to come in case we needed you."

"Not you. My goddess Cassany says it will help save you all from the king's wrath. Is that true or is she lying to me again?"

"It's true. He is the son of the king. His death will not go down well for us." Fia said.

"Someone is approaching." Thessa said as she pointed down the road.

"It's Danton's guards." Zedy said. "They are returning. I will use my flute and send them in circles for a bit." He produced his flute and sauntered off.

Thessa went to the corpse. She knew what to do and she used her magic instinctively to do it. She could feel the prince stir beneath her hands. She had done it. She had revived him.

Danton stretched awake, startled himself by looking at the blood on his leather armor, and then searched frantically for the dagger wound. He looked at Fia with wild eyes, and then he bolted off down the road toward where Zedy had his guards walking in circles.

"Should we go after him?" Thessa asked.

"Will he eventually come back after Arran?" Fia wondered.

"No, I made sure he has forgotten all that. He will not even remember how to get home to the king."

"Oh, then let him go." Fia said. "What harm can he do now?"

She is probably right.

"My cat agrees with you." Thessa said.

Fia's nose crinkled, "You keep saying that, but I didn't hear so much as a meow?"

"Oh, the cat is Sarren, the former Black Mage. I hear her in my mind."

Fia burst out in laughter, making Thessa smile. "I would ask how you convinced your goddess to do that to her, but I'm not sure I want to know."

"I told you. Cassany intercepted my travel spell the last time I saw you. We had an interesting meeting. I merely convinced her I needed an adviser. Sarren can't do any harm as a cat."

"Brilliant. I will have to ask Helious if I can do the same. I like pets." Sarren hissed at her intensely.

"She says she's not a pet."

"I figured out that one on my own." Fia said.

Zedy returned, "Well, that was strange. Danton ran right past his men, and they gave chase. I let them go. They are running in the wrong direction."

"Will they be all right?" Arran asked." I mean, they aren't going to run into the woods and starve or something, are they?"

Fia cooed, "Oh, look at you being all concerned for the man who was planning on killing you and taking your place."

We need to get going if you want to take the coin and go to the city.

"We will leave when I say, Sarren." She glanced around. "Any of you know how I get back to Emlestra?"

"You can take the river. Emlestra lies upon its shores to the south." Fia said. "I know where you can find a small boat. I can even take you there. I have been meaning to go that way. I have business down there." She turned to Arran, "That is if our business here is concluded?"

Arran nodded, "I think so. Zedy said he will help me complete the other tasks so I can continue my training. We are still going to head southwest to the Rister River." He took Fia's hand, "Thankyou and good luck with your training."

"And you get that power under control. If we three are to be allies, you need to be in total control."

"I will see to it, White Mage." Zedy assured her.

"I will." Arran agreed. "And you, Black Mage. I look forward to getting to know you better."

Thessa nodded, but she felt uncomfortable with the title. She supposed she would have to get used to it.

"Come, Thessa, the river and the boat are this way. Oh, and I know a handy water travel spell that will cut our travel time, unless you want to use your magic travel spell again."

"No, we will use yours!" Thessa said.

***

The small riverboat sped along the waters of the Tama river southward. Thessa had one of the rails of the boat in a death grip. "Do we have to be traveling so fast?"

"Are you worried? We are safe on the river. That is, unless we run into something solid."

Sarren was hidden under the seats. Thessa was surprised at her timidness.

Fia stood precariously to peer into the distance, which made Thessa's teeth hurt from clenching them, "Careful Fia. You will fall."

"Relax, I see our destination coming up." She pointed ahead. "Just in time too. There are only a few hours of daylight left."

Thessa squinted to see what looked to be docks extending out into the river. The city of Emlestra was hidden by a hill that extended up from the river embankment. "That's Emlestra?"

"Well, you can't see how big the city is from the river. It's over the hill and back a ways. If you want me to take you to a city on the water, Riverview down stream is right on top of the river."

"No, I am supposed to stop at Emlestra."

"In a few minutes, you will be, then."

Sarren came out of her hiding spot. *I hid the coin just off the main road to the city. I have several coins planted near the major cities. I will tell you all their locations.*

Thessa whispered into Sarren's furry ear, "Why? Don't you want them for yourself?"

You're in charge of my destiny now. It is in my best interest to make sure you are flush with money.

"I see your point."

"Is there any place special you would like me to dock?" Fia asked.

"No, I have never been here before that I can remember."

"Okay, this city is not for the weak-hearted. There are a lot of thieves and unlikeable people who roam these streets. You must be careful. The city has several inns and a really great marketplace where one can find just about anything, but just like big marketplaces, this one his full of swindlers and cheats."

"Sounds like a terrible place."

"Oh, it has its charms if you are careful and mind your money. In fact, keep it close to you and in front pockets if you can. It's easier to steal if it's kept in a purse." She steered the boat toward the bank. "Gather your things. We are almost there.

Chapter 5
The Meeting

"Marlee!" Ephaltus beckoned. "Where is that apprentice of mine?" He entered the Ocularius Magnus room and found her engrossed with a vision of one of the six mages. She was giggling and obviously not hearing his calls. He sauntered up behind her and peered into the lens. It wasn't the vision of the Green Mage using her magic wastefully entreating a vine to play with a great ginger cat that suddenly enraged him. No, it was the eyeball in the fringe edge of the enormous lens. He pulled Marlee forcefully from the seat ignoring her startled protests and he sent the Oculus spinning causing the image to fade to black.

"Ephaltus! Are you listening to me! Why did you pull me away like that? You frazzled my wits!"

Ephaltus turned to her, still fuming," Such a silly way to say I frightened you, and frankly, I don't care if I did. Did you forget to calibrate this infernal thing again?"

"Well, I thought I did." Marlee said.

"As I expected. I just saw one of the gods or their servants was watching. I caught the culprit peeking into the side lens. That's it! I am putting my foot down this time." He cleared his throat. Gather yourself and put on something fitting. "We are going to Hearthhaven."

"Marlee almost forgot to breathe for a moment and the air rushed back to her in a gasp. We are going to meet with the gods?"

"Oh, don't be so dramatic. They are deities, but they are not *the* gods, not the ones who created this world. They are a bunch of spoiled offspring who have nothing better to do than cheat."

"Why do they take such an interest in the tournament?"

"Well, the winner is the ruler, and the god of the ruler is usually the one who's pushed on the rest of the kingdoms. It's a bit of a strategy, this cheating. You see, the other gods find it necessary to thwart Cassany. They are afraid the kingdoms will plunge into darkness under Cassany's rule or worship, and it probably will."

"Isn't that a good thing? We should allow them to defeat the god of darkness."

"No, we are supposed to make this fair. We cannot allow favor or exclusion of anyone. It's our job. The tournament must be fair, no matter the consequence. Besides, it falls in our favor too."

"Our favor?"

Ephaltus cleared his throat again, "I just mean it's easier on us if everything is fair. Can you imagine how the tournament might go if we took sides?" Marlee gave him a blank, contemplating expression. "You'll find out what I mean all in good time."

"What do I wear to meet gods?"

Ephaltus was even more irritated," Dress as if you were meeting a king on his throne."

"I don't have anything so grand as that!" she said.

"I don't know what to tell you then. Just get ready to leave. I want to get there as soon as possible."

***

Ephaltus entered the chamber of the gods and headed directly for the long, wooden council table. He made himself comfortable sitting in one of the end seats, waiting for the meeting to begin. Helious was the first deity to arrive. It was no wonder Helios was early; his great dragon wings carried him swiftly to the meeting place. He shifted forms into a bearded, older gentleman with golden hair and golden robes to match. His face appeared sun kissed, and his golden eyes sparkled with the brilliance of the sun.

"Ephaltus." The god of the White Mage said in greeting.

"Helious." Ephaltus acknowledged.

Asrion entered the chamber next. His dark hair and blue eyes were accented perfectly by his ironic blue robes, ironic due to the fact he was the god of the Grey Mage. He glanced at Ephaltus, almost sneering before he took his place next to Helious. "Helious, brother. Good to see you." He said without so much as glancing toward Ephaltus.

"You as well, brother." Helious said.

Ephaltus sighed and Asrion stopped for a moment to glare at him. He opened his mouth to say something, something snide no doubt, when Andiel, goddess of the Red Mage, entered the room. She appeared as a nice-looking old woman, which grey hair and sparkling blue eyes. She smiled widely at the other two gods and then slipped into the seat next to Ephaltus. "Well met, Tourney Master," she said in a sweet, melodic voice. Everyone loved Andiel. She was like the perfect grandmother, giving, caring, and sweet natured, unless she was crossed, then she would show her true and awesome power. But no one ever crossed that line on purpose.

"Andiel, how lovely to see you." Asrion said.

"Yes, you look well." Helious chimed in.

"Helious, Asrion," she said with a nod." It always fills my heart with joy to see you two."

Benera and Nateria walked into the room together. An odd pairing considering their champions, the Blue Mage, and the Green Mage, are rivals and immune to most of each other's magic. The two goddesses should be at odds, but they weren't. Instead, they were getting on as if they were best friends. Benera was laughing at something Nateria said as they both took their seats.

"She won't come." Asrion was saying to Helious, "She never does."

"Don't be so negative." Andiel cautioned. "I asked her here myself. She would not deny me."

"So, she is running around as a female this century, then." Helious stated.

"For now." Asrion said, "Give her a few days and she will be bragging about how great she portrays a male. I find the gender swapping thing tedious. I say make up your damn mind and stick with it."

"Hear, hear!" Helious agreed.

"Now boys. You know Cassany enjoys the attention. Why not give it to her?" Andiel said.

"Because it's weird and unusual." Asrion said flatly. He looked at Ephaltus as if seeing him for the first time." Wouldn't you say tourney master?"

"Don't drag me into this," he said.

"No, I want to hear your thoughts on the matter." Asrion insisted.

"All right," Ephaltus breathed in sharply, clearly not wanting to weigh in on the matter. "You gods are all shadows of your parents, the old gods, and bickering on about each other should be beneath you, but here we are."

"How dare you!" Asrion said.

"Oh, blow it out your ear." Ephaltus muttered.

"Why, I should smite you where you stand." Asrion said.

"Well, I'm sitting, genius."

Helious shrank away slightly, shaking his head. Ephaltus saw him give Andiel a sorrowful, worried glance.

"I am going to teach you some respect, tourney master!" Asrion said.

"I would like to see you try, you pompous old windbag."

Asrion stood up.

Ephaltus smirked, "Careful Asrion, with all your smarts, philosophies, and mental faculties, you think you would remember the last time you tried to show me up."

"Asrion, please sit down." Andiel said." Ephaltus, please stop antagonizing him."

Asrion hesitated and then sat backdown. "We will be rid of you soon enough."

Ephaltus glanced around, "Yes you will, and where is my apprentice by the way?"

Marlee had a piece of parchment and was talking intently to Nateria. Knowing her sister was the goddesses' Green Mage made him a little uncomfortable about it. What was his apprentice discussing so fervently? He was about to find out when he spotted the black smoke rising from a widening black hole in the floor. He pointed to the spot to alert the other nearby gods, "There she is. Cassany's portal spell."

Asrion glanced at the widening hole and smoke, "So dramatic, as usual."

"Be nice, Asrion." Andiel scolded.

The black smoke wafted through the air until the figure of a woman stepped out of it. The smoke cleared and Cassany floated to the seat beside Asrion, who groaned at realizing the goddess wanted to sit beside him. Marlee came to sit next to Ephaltus, and he welcomed her company. He would have to ask her what she was talking to Nateria about later.

Ephaltus stood from his end seat and held up his hand for silence. "Good, you are all here. Now, I will get straight to the point. I know you are all looking through the Oculus at your champions to gain an advantage. What will I have to do to make you all stop?"

"To whom are you referring exactly, Tourney Master? I have not looked through your spy glass." Asrion said. "I'm not at all certain how something like that is even done."

"What possible advantage could spying on our champions give us?" Benera asked. "I can already see my champion without your contraption."

"No, no, no," Ephaltus shook his head." Don't play coy. You know I am not talking about watching your own champion. I am talking about spying on the competition and possibly plotting to sabotage them."

"Perhaps it's good you are set to retire, tourney master, your paranoia is appalling." Helious stated.

"Is this the reason we have been summoned here? If so, I have better things to do." Asrion said as he stood up.

"No, please sit back down, Asrion." Andiel said. "I am afraid there is another matter we must discuss. There is an anomaly in the selection process."

"What kind of anomaly?" Nateria asked.

"The former White Mage, Zedy, has accidentally become the White Mage again."

"What! Impossible." Helious said. "I would have sensed it."

"See, you have been looking!" Ephaltus accused Andiel. "How could you have known otherwise?"

"All right, yes, I have been sneaking a look here and there." Andiel said. "Now that you know, I would thank you to shut up about it and let me speak."

"Why did you do it, Andiel?" Ephaltus asked, while sitting back in his chair.

Andiel glanced around the room at the face of her brothers and sisters before answering. "I have always been honest with you all. The fact is my champion is a sweet and kind-hearted woman and it's about time we had a good calm leader for a change. I don't want any more of your horrible champions to win anymore. I have always played by the book, and I have very few champions to show for it."

"What of my champion?" came a demure voice from beside Asrion. It was Cassany, and she was speaking in low tones.

"Oh, speak up, Cassany. We know that demure voice and pleasant manner you're displaying is just an act." Asrion said.

Andiel pursed her lips, "I would say your champion is a good one too, Cass, but I know what you will end up doing to her in the end."

"Why? Who's her champion?" Nateria asked.

Asrion huffed, "As if you don't know. All of you are so tiresome. We have been at this for hundreds of years. We all know each other's tricks and mannerisms."

"I really don't know. You pompous fool!"

"Oh, name calling already, Nateria?"

"Stop it, the both of you." Andiel said. "Nateria, Cass's champion is a tragic one. She is the daughter of my champion. A former blood feeder who Cass has manipulated before and will again."

"Your champion's daughter! Is that allowed, Tourney Master?" Helious asked.

"I know of no rule against it." Ephaltus replied.

"Could we get back to the matter at hand?" Andiel directed.

"There is no rule against a former Mage rom taking another go round, is there?" Benera said.

"Technically no," Ephaltus said. "but I think I know what Andiel is getting at here. Zedy was a mage long ago. He is experienced and will probably run circles around your new recruits. He is now a reviewer and training Arran. Does that give the Blue Mage an unfair advantage?"

"I don't believe so." Benera said.

"Of course not, Benera, The Blue Mage is your champion. Nateria pointed out.

"We knew this would happen one day." Asrion said. "We let the former mages keep their abilities and now there are several of them running around."

"What do you propose? Andiel?"

"What if we evened the odds by allowing each mage to train with an older one?"

"I can't sanction that." Asrion said. "I think we should leave everything as itis. If each god wants a champion to train their mage, so be it. It's just part of the process."

Chapter 6
Tanyth Veridian

Cassany had secretly instructed the former Black Mage, Sarren, to report on Thessa's progress at regular intervals. The transport spell was not particularly difficult at Sarren's present size and weight, and she almost used too much magic and overshot the mountain hideaway of the winged goddess. When she did arrive, she found Cassany waiting for her in the goddess's favorite sitting room. A replica of the six kingdom's throne room, complete with a slightly different customized throne to suit Cassany's extravagant tastes.

For a long moment after Sarren entered the room, Cassany sat staring at her. Cassany's reddish black eyes made Sarren extremely uncomfortable. She looked down, but she could feel the goddess's eyes still upon her.

"Did they see you leave the boat?"

No, they think I am cowering underneath the seats.

"Good." Cassany said. The goddess stared at Sarren but said nothing further, which made Sarren extremely nervous. Thankfully, the awkward silence was broken when the door to the throne room opened and in stepped a tall man dressed in black animal hide. He wore a hood to hide his face and Sarren was surprised he was allowed to enter the chamber in the presence of a goddess with a sword strapped to his side and a bow and quiver on his back. He stepped a few paces in front of the throne and took a knee, bowing his head to Cassany.

"Rise Tanyth Veridian." Cassany said in a booming, yet feminine voice.

The man called Tanyth rose to his feet and removed the hood from his head. *He is an elf!* Sarren observed.

Cassany's eyes darted to Sarren, and she sank down, wondering if the goddess was reluctant of her presence.

"My goddess, I am here to serve thee." Tanyth said.

"Good, and if I tell you I want you to kill the Black Mage and take her place, would you object?"

Tanyth smirked, "Why should I object?"

Cassany chuckled, "Because the Black Mage has my power. She will not be a pushover. You will not be able to use many of your assassin skills on her. She will sense your intentions, feel your malice, and detect your lies. She is just as likely to kill you as you are to kill her."

"You underestimate me, my goddess. I only use blunt ways of assassination on fools. I have more skill than perhaps you realize; furthermore, I am an elf. Let her try to detect me, I say."

"I admire your confidence, but don't be a fool."

"There is nothing foolish about me, my goddess. But, if I may, it is sheer speculation and folly to postulate on how I may have fared against your champion, for you know I am unable to kill the Black Mage and take her place. You know of my condition."

Cassany eyed him, "Yes, well, pity. It would have been a spectacular fight." She tossed her hand flippantly, "Anyway, I cannot interfere with the Black Mage's power. It is forbidden by decree the gods, not to mention by the codes of the tournament. The rules also say I am not to interfere with the other mages either. I am afraid I must train and accept who I have no matter how difficult she may be to control."

"Rules of the gods and tournament? Since when have rules stopped you before, my goddess? There are ways around my condition, you know. I can also kill the other mages in ways that do not require my direct hand."

Cassany's expression brightened, "Can you do it, then?"

"I can."

Cassany's mood became almost cheerful, "Why not? The other gods certainly interfere. I have caught them on more than one occasion." She clasped her hands together. "You will not receive any help from me. You will have to do this all on your own, you understand?"

"Naturally." Tanyth said. "But how will your champion react?"

"That's just it. It doesn't matter. Thessa will never know I was involved."

"You do not tell your champion information that will help her?"

"Not yet. She still needs — some work." Cassany glanced at Sarren. "But I do have a plan in place with her. She will come around. I may have to bend the rules a bit, but I will break her."

"As you wish." Tanyth bowed slightly.

"I cannot divulge your target's location, but I know he is in hiding. I think the fool believes he is still normal."

"How shall I find him then?"

"I can give you a lead on his whereabouts. I have a connection with him."

At first Sarren thought Cassany planned to get rid of Thessa, then she suspected they were no longer talking about the Black Mage when the conversation shifted. She only knew that somehow Cassany was marking one or more mages for death. Sarren suspected it must be Hana, the Red Mage, because of her connection with Thessa. At least she hoped it was Hana!

"Once the deed is done, we will lay all this at our champion's feet. Thessa will not embrace her destiny so easily. I will therefore drag her to it kicking and screaming!" She turned to Sarren. "Come here, Sarren."

Sarren pulled herself up, and nimbly bounded to the throne, her paws felt so light and dexterous.

"I shall employee Sarren, the Black Mage's servant. Sarren will find a way to lead Thessa to your ultimate target. I want her present when you have your target exterminated."

"If I may ask, why?"

"I want to see if Thessa will try to interfere. It would also be a bonus if Thessa were blamed for the deed. A reputation as a killer would do her good. I think it would go a long way to breaking her of her bad habits."

"Shall I frame her, then?"

Cassany thought for a long moment, "No, I don't think so. If it so happens she gets blamed then so be it, but I believe framing her might send her down a different path. One where she is bent on clearing her name instead of feeling the blame as a mere injustice. She will blame herself for the first target you are to find. I made certain of that."

"Ah, I see."

"When you are able, I also would like you to stay close to Thessa, away in the shadows. She is about to see the world in a whole different light, and it might be good to throw an obstacle or two in her path to hone her skills and keep her sharp."

"Understood."

"Wait." Cassany looked off into the distance. "I sense the one you seek has made his first kill. You had better hurry along before some townsfolk somewhere misunderstands."

"I shall travel at once, my goddess." Tanyth watched as the door to the chambers opened just a crack. He took the hint for him to vacate. He reached for the door, but it slammed shut before he could open it further. Tanyth turned to see the goddess with her arm outstretched. "Was there something more?" Tanyth asked.

Cassany lowered her arm, "I just wanted to remind you."

"Yes, my goddess?"

"Black Mage's often change their appearance and as a result attract a lot of attention, they are ill equipped to handle. Do you understand?"

"Yes, I think so. If Thessa makes herself beautiful, men will take notice, and she probably has not thought about such a thing before. She will make herself beautiful for her own sake not to attract the opposite sex, so she will be surprised when they begin to flock around her. I have seen this happen before, my goddess."

"Exactly!"

"Your point?" Tanyth asked.

"A simple one, remember always this is not a love story. It's a tragedy." Tanyth grinned and then turned once more toward the door. It opened for him, and he exited.

Sarren sat watching as the goddess shifted her wings to fit the back of the throne.

"Now that you know of my plans, and you know Thessa a bit better, what do you think." She asked.

Sarren tried to talk, and it came out as a meow.

Cassany waved her hand and Sarren was back to her human self. "Speak now."

"I... I think she will have a hard time doing your bidding." Sarren said.

"Hmm, do you know why I allowed Thessa to resurrect you and you not become a blood feeder as you should have become?"

"I wouldn't presume to understand your ways, my goddess."

"Because I was concerned being a blood feeder, a vampire, would impede your ability to train Thessa. From the moment I whispered into Thessa's ear in the Cavern of the Winged Goddess, for her to resurrect you, I have had the intention of you training her. She might have believed the thought was her own, but it was not. So, now you know." She raised her hand and transformed Sarren back into a cat. "It is your job to make her do my bidding. Should you fail, your fate will be much worse than becoming a blood feeder. Now go back to her and do keep in mind how your life, or unlife, may be if you are unable to convince her to be the best Black Mage she can possibly be, understood?"

Sarren let out a demure mew.

"Good!" Cassany flit her wrist and Sarren was instantly returned to the boat where she left Thessa and Fia. Sarren yowled out in surprise at the abrupt teleportation.

"Shut up, you stupid cat. It's not like I have ever crashed a speeding boat. You are safe!" Fia said. Sarren settled down and returned to her spot beneath Thessa's seat.

Before the boat reached the dock, Fia slowed the boat down and sang a peculiar song compelling fish to jump from the river into her waiting basket. She looked at the hungry Sarren, "I usually have men falling over themselves to clean my catch for me but seeing there are no men I will have to do it myself." She chucked one of the smaller fish underneath the seat to Sarren and the cat bit into the succulent flesh ravenously. She dragged her prize further under the seat, complete with a covetous growl. Sarren continued to devour her fish.

Fia jumped out of the boat and pulled it to shore, dragging it up onto the bank. "We might as well have a meal together before you go into the city. It might be difficult for you to find lodging this late in the day and that means you will probably not have time to find something to eat."

"Thank you. You have thought of everything." Thessa said.

"I just realized we can't fry the fish without something to fry it on." Fia said. "Roast it on the end of a stick?" Thessa suggested.

"I thought of that, but the flesh will come apart when it cooks, dropping the meat into the fire."

"Smoke it then?"

"Do you have an entire day to waste? The city is only about twenty minutes away."

"I guess not." Thessa answered.

"Wait, I have a small piece of armor, big enough to sit on the coals and fry some fish. Why didn't I think of it before?" She went to her saddle bag in the boat and produced a small piece of plate mail. She returned to the fire and began heating it up. "If you will help me fillet the fish, we can eat faster and be on our way."

Thessa nodded and produced her best dagger.

Chapter 7
The City

F ia maneuvered the boat into the docks of Emlestra. She tied it off and prepared to disembark.

"Well, Thessa. I guess this is where we part for now."

"I can't think you enough for your help, Fia." Thessa said.

"Will you be okay in the city by yourself?"

"I remembered after thinking about it that I may have passed through here a long time ago, but I don't remember much. I wasn't exactly thinking clearly back then. I will be fine. I have Sarren with me." The cat jumped out of the boat.

"Oh yes, I forgot about her." She smiled and Thessa got the feeling she really had not forgotten the cat.

"When will I see you again? Are you staying in the city long?"

Fia seemed anxious about answering. "I won't be here long, no. Once I finish my business, I will be heading back to Maslah's camp."

Thessa was not sure what she meant, and Fia must have seen it in her face.

"Maslah is my father. His camp is home."

"Oh, okay."

Fia reached in to give Thessa a hug and she stiffened like a board while the White Mage embraced her. "Not used to hugs I see."

Thessa snickered awkwardly, "No, sorry. I will have to work on that one some more. I think the only one who has ever hugged me is my mother, my true mother that is."

"Well, you will like them once you get used to them. Ta-ta for now." She waved.

"What?"

"That's a nice, non-permanent way to say goodbye."

"Oh, Ta-ta then."

Fia smiled and bounded off down the dock, leaving Thessa and Sarren to find their own way to the city.

Thessa entered Emlestra proper just after sundown with Sarren chasing after. The river flowed noisily to the east of the gates. The coin Sarren had left was in a tin box near a tree just slightly out of the way of the main road. It took only a few minutes to dig it up.

When inside the gates, the city patrons had taken to the streets in celebration and could be heard even over the roaring rapids of the river. Thessa couldn't help but smile at the goings on. There were people obviously taken with drink, and others enjoying the dances of the city folk spurred on by the lively music being played by a merry throng of minstrels. There were young girls holding sticks with ribbons tied to them, which flowed behind them, as they ran together crisscross in the streets. Boys chased after them as if they were going to snatch the ribbons away from them. The older boys and girls joined in the dances. The elders sat along the street's edges in foldable wooden chairs stretched with canvas. Thessa had seen such chairs in her youth on the beaches. She looked at the shops to see if she could find the numismatist's place of business. She saw the sign of the coin collector not far down the street behind a crowd of seated elder folk. One of them was bound to be the numismatist. She hoped she could tear him or her away from the festivities long enough to look at her coin. She needed the money to secure lodging.

She stopped along the way to peer at herself in a shop window. She had to make sure the beauty spell was holding, even though she knew it was. For some reason, she didn't trust the magic. Her brown eyes stared back at her in the dimming light of the setting sun, her features were captivating from her dimples to her beautiful pale complexion. She was stunning to behold, even to herself. She raised her chin and wandered over to the older crowd.

"Hello, I don't mean to bother you all, but I wonder if you know the person who owns the coin shop?"

An older man with a short white beard and deep laugh lines around his eyes smiled at her, "That would be me, but I have closed the shop for the festival, I'm afraid. You will have to come back tomorrow." He put the stem of his pipe in his mouth and took a long puff.

"I would, but you see, I'm new here and I need to sell this coin, or I will be sleeping in the alley tonight."

The coin shop owner glanced at one of his friends, "It's always a dire story."

"Excuse me?" Thessa asked, slightly offended.

"I'll tell you what. Why don't you show me this coin of yours and I will see if it's worth anything to me."

Thessa could tell he was hoping it was junk so he could just turn her away and be done with it. She took out the ancient coin and held it up for him.

"Well, you are going to have to bring it closer. My old eyes can't see that far away in the dimming light," he said.

Thessa held it closer, and the old man held out his hand. Thessa hesitated, not wanting to just hand it over to a stranger. He stared at her, his eyes widening in an expression of impatience.

"Well?" he said.

Thessa handed him the coin. After he examined it for a moment, he got excited and sat up. He looked at Thessa and then immediately calmed down and resumed his relaxed posture.

"It's rare alright, but not worth much. We can go to my shop, and I will give you something for it."

"Excuse me, sir, but you were extremely excited when you first saw it. Are you sure you want to shortchange me?" Thessa could feel the man's heart race when he first laid eyes on the coin, and it had not subsided despite his now calm demeanor.

"I am not sure I understand your tone, young lady," he said.

"It's easy if you try. I want the full worth of the coin, sir," she said. "Nothing less."

"Of course, I will give you it's full worth, such that it is, when we get to my shop."

"Thessa could tell he was still planning on giving her far less than the coin was worth, but she nodded anyway so she could get him into the shop and away from the prying eyes of the man's friends.

"Ah, here we are." The man said as he produced a key to the front door of the shop signed Coin Exchange. Smoke from his pipe lifted above his head in a white-grey cloud. The solid wooden door creaked slightly as the man pushed it open. A bell rang out when the door bumped into it. Thessa entered behind the owner. He pushed the door closed locking it again. Thessa gave him a worried gaze. He must have sensed her concern.

"Oh, I am closed, and I don't want anyone wandering in. You are quite safe with me."

Thessa nodded. Inwardly, she knew she was far safer with him than he was with her.

He rounded a glass and wood countertop and proceeded to light one of the lanterns nearby with a long-stemmed piece of straw he lit by placing the end in his pipe and inhaling to excite the burn of his tobacco. He turned back to Thessa and placed his pipe on the counter in a small, worn wooden holder. Wisps of smoke snaked up from its bowl. He took out an eyepiece and examined the coin, then he took down the lantern and examined it even closer with it bathed in light.

"It's rare. I will give you two gold magi for it."

Thessa coughed uneasily. "Sir, I know it's worth. That coin is easily worth one hundred gold magi pieces. What are you trying to pull over on me?" She blinked as she stared at the man's exposed neck. Something within her made her instincts flare, and she very nearly lurched at him. She was no longer a blood feeder. It must have been the resurfacing of the old habit.

The old man coughed, "Well, I can give you twenty." A bead of sweat appeared on his brow.

"Thank you, no. I will travel to the next town." She reached for the coin and the man recoiled. She grew more determined and reached again. The man pulled back even farther. Thessa felt her face become hot. Her breathing was shallow and calculated. The veins in his neck pulsated as she leaned into the urge to strike.

Her expression must have been convincing because his eyes had a tinge of fear in them and he relented, "All right, you win, I will give you eighty gold magi."

"Eighty-five." She was relieved that the tension had subsided.

"All right, eighty-five if you need to feel like I treated you more fairly. I do have to make a profit too, you know."

"You will." Thessa stated blankly.

The man smacked his lips and muttered something under his breath as he turned to go to the back room.

"Leave the coin here on the counter, please." Thessa said.

"The man feigned irritation and left the coin on the counter as he slipped into the back room. Thessa saw a light appear where the man obviously lit a lamp or lantern. A mere moment later and the man appeared with Thessa's gold. He reluctantly handed the leather pouch of coins to her. She dumped them out on the counter and carefully counted them before she replaced them in the pouch and cinched it closed. "Nice doing business with you."

The man grumbled and managed a weak grin. "Who are you, anyway?"

"Me? I'm nobody," she replied.

"Your eyes. You look as though you could benefit from a good meal."

"Thanks for the observation. Perhaps you had better not comment further." She was anticipating the old familiar critique of her unusual appearance.

"I meant nothing by it. I was just going to suggest the Suckling Pig.

"The what?"

The man broke the building apprehension with an unexpected hardy laugh, "It's the inn at the edge of the main street. The proprietor is a friend and I send her business when I can."

"Oh, yes, thank you." *That was awkward,* she thought. *He must get kickbacks.* "I will visit the place."

"Good, good." The man said rubbing his hands on his shirt nervously, while he uncomfortably glanced around looking for something else to say.

Thessa wasted no time leaving the numismatist's shop. The Suckling Pig would work for her. She didn't care. She just wanted to get to an inn for a nice meal and a bed.

Your guise has dropped. Sarren said in her head.

"Oh, how do I keep it going?"

You can't let things get to you. Stress will sometimes make the appearance spell drop. You must remember to keep it going in times of stress.

"I will try. I am too tired to try again tonight. I will just leave it for now.

The Suckling Pig Inn was much nicer than she had thought it would be. The common room was well kept and there was a roaring fire in the fireplace. I minstrel sang in the comfortable lounging area as a well-dressed maiden served drinks. Thessa approached the counter.

"Well, you look like you have been through it!" The woman behind the counter said, and Thessa shrank back a bit. "Oh, she means nothing by that." A portly man said, pushing the woman aside. "Go on, Sienna, let me tend to the customers at the counter." Sienna grunted and wandered off toward what looked to be the kitchen. "Sorry about that. Sienna owns the place, but she has no business savvy."

Thessa nodded uneasily.

"She doesn't know people." He paused as if Thessa was supposed to reply. When she did not, he went on. "What can I do for you? A room perhaps? A meal? You do look a bit undernourished."

"Both actually, and I wonder if I could have the meal brought up to my room?" She was not all that hungry due to Fia's fish meal, but she ordered for appearances.

"Certainly! We aim to please here at the Suckling Pig. I would understand why you wouldn't want to eat here in the commons, people's prying eyes and all."

"Why would I mind that?" Thessa asked.

"You know." He leaned in closer so he could whisper, "Your appearance."

Thessa looked down at her shabby attire. Once the spell dropped, she was reminded that she had not cleaned up much since the dirty water of the cavern where she had been left by her mother and Asleth. In fact, the rust-colored spots on her blouse were probably faded blood. "Can you launder my clothes?"

"I can. I can also have some new clothes brought up for you, assuming you can pay for all this." A look of concern appeared on his face. "By the way, how are you going to pay for all this?"

Thessa opened the pouch with the gold and took out a gold magi. She glanced up at the innkeeper just in time to see him hide his surprise. Perhaps she shouldn't have advertised to him she had a full pouch of gold. She quickly cinched the pouch and tucked it away. "I assume this will do?"

"Yes, indeed." The innkeeper said. "This and you have change coming."

"No, use it to buy my clothes and for the laundry service. I would like two meals, one tonight, and the other tomorrow morning. You may keep the rest."

The innkeeper nodded happily and turned to a peg board behind him. "One key? Are you expecting anyone else?"

"No, one key is fine." She thought it was odd for him to ask. Maybe it was common practice.

He gave her the key to room number six. "Room six, up the stairs and to the left." He pointed to the stairway. "The numbers are painted over so you will have to look hard at them. I will have Sienna bring up a tray for you in say ten minutes?"

"Yes, ten minutes would be fine." She said as she gathered herself and made her way to the stairs. She felt the innkeeper's eyes on her the entire way to the top.

The room at the Suckling Pig was as nice as the rest of the inn. Well maintained and clean, the room consisted of a washbasin, a good-sized bed, a small table with two chairs, two lanterns for light, and a chest of drawers with a large mirror on the wall behind it. She sat on the bed and found it to be comfortable. She laid back on it and started to drift off until her stomach growled. She was hungrier than she thought. The fish meal did not stick with her long, it seemed. A knock at the door and Thessa let in Sienna with a tray of food. Once the woman was gone, Thessa dug into the roast chicken and potatoes, tossing Sarren a scrap of meat here and there. Before long, another knock at the door brought a new set of clothes. Thessa was dumbfounded at how the innkeeper knew her size, but assumed it was due to his expertise at guessing what his patrons wanted. Thessa donned a soft robe and let the girl who brought her new clothes take the old clothes for laundering.

The clothes were a bit odd. The black dress was made of solid fabric, but it still felt silky. The dress also had thin bands of fabric for the arms and legs. She had seen the style in the city before, and she felt it left little to cover the midsection. The top was a metallic, leafy fabric, which unnaturally conformed to any way you molded it. She put the odd clothing aside. She would have to deal with it later. She was not about to wear something like that out in public.

She prepared for bed by brushing her hair with the brush provided by the inn. She paused at the mirror for a long moment to gaze into her gaunt face. She did look malnourished.

Chapter 8
Clever Secrets

The Green Mage, Teoni, poured over the book she had stolen from the Arsenal of the Way. Surrounding her were her beloved plants. Vines of green and gold snaked up into the corners of her bedchamber. The ceiling opened to let the sunshine in and provide light for both her plants and her reading endeavors. Other, more dangerous, plants writhed in the corner and there were even smaller plants lurking in the corners on shelves.

Teoni was engrossed in her reading when one of the vines reached down from above the window to touch her shoulder. She started upright and caressed the vine, "What do you sense out there?" She crossed the room to peer out the window. Although the path was well lit, it was still difficult to see through the thick plant life. She raised her hands and commanded the plants to give her a clear view of the pathway to her abode. She flinched when she saw the darkened figure of a man or woman hidden in the shade behind one of her bushes. She blinked, and the shadow was gone.

She whispered to the vine closest to her, "Better prepare for the worst. I think we have a visitor." The plant made a low humming noise. "I know the Blue Mage isn't afraid of the light. What are you saying?" The plant hummed again. "Ah, the creature stays in the shadows. Well, that is good news. It must be bringing word from the Black Mage, then." The plant hummed again. "No, it doesn't matter. The Black Mage and her minions always exude darkness and danger. It's common. Don't worry about it. I know she is traditionally our enemy." The vine's humming intensified. "All right, if it makes you feel better, go ahead with the precautions." The vine rippled back. Teoni craned her head to see the position of the sun. "There are still about six hours of sunlight left. As long as we have the sun, we have power." She looked at her lunar calendar, "And the moon is full tonight. The lunar plants are at their zenith too. We are perfectly fine." The vines recoiled back into their position on the window seal.

Teoni went back to her book. She felt a pang of regret at her betrayal of her sister Marlee. She reread the passage where it stated Marlee would take her place as the Tourney Master apprentice while she took over the mantle of the Green Mage. "I hope this passage is correct. I must find a way to see if Marlee is indeed Ephaltus's apprentice," she said. She gazed at one of her golden vines as it twisted to get a better position under the sunlight. "I just don't have the courage to confront either of them yet. Of course, I'm sure Marlee is watching me through the Ocularius Magnus." She closed the book. "Do you suppose one of your plants can find a way into the arena and find out if she is the apprentice for me?" The plants hummed. "Yes, I don't know why I didn't ask before. Thank you, my friends!" She sat back in her chair, somewhat relieved. "I suppose we can have the midday meal," she said.

The plants brought fruits and berries from the outside into the room. Teoni fed insects and small rodents to the flesh-eating plants still writhing in the corner before she sat down to partake of the bounty the plants had given her. "Thank you, my friends, for the abundance you give me. We feast upon the flesh of plants and the fruits of our labor to make us strong." She began to eat.

After the midday meal, she watered her plants and retired out into the garden. Vines from various plants were always near her, no matter where she went on the grounds. She liked to go to the garden to train with her abilities, shapeshifting into bunnies and foxes in order to frolic amongst the hedges and bushes. But today she just wanted to enjoy the sanctuary and oversee the preparations for the intruder. She was not worried about the creature stalking her. She received no ill feelings from it. Until, at last, she felt the presence of something behind her. The sun was setting low on the horizon and the shadows of the garden were growing longer. The hair on the back of her neck began to stand up, and she turned to see who or what approached. In the garden, which was still drenched in sunlight, stood a tall man wearing all black. His hair was jet black and his complexion a deep olive. She noticed his ears protruding out from under his hair were slightly long and pointed. He was an elf.

"Hello? Who might you be?" She asked.

"I am called Tanyth, Green Mage." The elf said flatly.

"Is it you who has been skulking about my gardens?"

"Yes."

"Has the Black Mage sent you?"

"No."

"Well then, out with it, what do you want?"

"You are not the one the goddess wants."

Teoni was amused, "Oh, is that so? Which goddess do you speak for, then?"

"My goddess, Cassany."

"Cassany, oh? I thought you were not sent by the Black Mage."

"I have not been. The goddess and Black Mage are not one and the same."

"Then why would Cassany send you here to me?"

"How dare you question her!" The elf made a step forward and the plant life surrounding them both moved in closer. Tanyth stopped and stared at the plants in surprise.

"Careful, you are in my garden and my friends do not like irrational elves. Your response tells me you are a zealot of Cassany. Okay, I am currently going against the tradition of being allied against the Blue Mage, Arran. Surely you know that. I have not taken any steps against the Black Mage, and she should also be an ally of Arran."

"Yes," he said. "She is."

"What manner of elf are you? I have never seen one with your skin tone before."

"I am a dark elf."

"A dark elf. Yes, I should have realized, knowing how Cassany is the mistress of dark places. You still have not answered my question. What do you want of me?"

"Cassany is thinking ahead to the tournament, and she tells me you are not the one." The vegetation moved in closer.

"Not the one for what? Are you referring to my sister, Marlee? Yes, I took her power and switched places with her. I was only trying to protect her. She is better off now with the Tourney Master."

"No lies!" The dark elf was examining the surrounding plants carefully.

"It is no lie. I love my sister and I wanted to see her safe. Who are you?" Teoni was becoming a bit alarmed now, and the plants responded to her feelings of dread by moving in even closer.

Tanyth drew a dagger, and the plants went wild, moving in to wrap Teoni up in vines so that no blade could penetrate them to get to her.

"What is your plan? You want to kill me and take my place as the Green Mage?"

"No." Tanyth said. He remained still. "I cannot do that."

"If you kill me, elf, that's what will happen. You will become the Green Mage."

"No, I won't. You have to be one among the living for that to happen and I am... am something else. If I were to kill a mage, I will not take their place."

"Then why are you here with a dagger threatening me?"

"I will not kill you even though I am able to if I want."

"How can you kill a mage then if you would not take the mage's place? You are acting strange. Are you here for medicine? Do you need one of my cures? Is that it?"

"I have a way."

"A way to what? Kill a mage?"

"Yes."

"I think you had better leave, elf. I don't think I like this conversation. You are acting as if you are out of your right mind. I believe if Cassany has created someone who can assassinate the mages for her own gain, the other gods and goddesses will not let that stand for long."

"Perhaps, but for now, they don't know about me." He took a step closer to the Green Mage, who was continuing to be wrapped in strong vines.

Tanyth smirked, hesitated, and then put away his dagger. He turned and took a leaf between his fingers, rubbing the soft leaf absently as if nothing had occurred.

"What are you doing?" Teoni asked. "I said you should leave this place."

"I am not here to kill you, Green Mage. I am here; however, to show you that I am able to kill you. Cassany requires a favor of you."

"Cassany can go to the two hells for all I care. How dare you come here and threaten me!"

Tanyth stiffened at Teoni's blasphemy. "If not you, there will be another. You will grant my goddess her favor or I will end you with a replacement who will. It's up to you, but I suggest you heed my warning. It is not a threat I make to you. I am prepared to follow through with my words."

Teoni allowed the vines surrounding her to loosen and subside, "What favor?"

Tanyth turned to face her with a growing grin on his lips. "A poison. Cassany wishes you to make me a strong poison. Once that can kill rapidly. You can make such a poison from plants, can you not?"

"Yes, I can, but the question is will I? What purpose does a god have for a poison?"

"I will pay you handsomely for the poison." Tanyth said.

"Is it to kill a mage?"

"No, I don't need poison for that. The poison will not be used to kill anyone."

"I'm confused. You want me to make a strong poison and then you are not going to use it to kill. Are you using it to threaten?"

"No, if you must know, it is for someone with a god-like constitution. It will only make him sick. No poison is strong enough to kill him. He will live on after the effects wear off."

"Well, I suppose it would do no harm but no, I will not make you a poison no matter what your intentions may be or for any price. I want you to turn around and leave this place, now!"

"Are you certain? You may come to regret this decision."

"Will you leave on your own or do I have to force you out?" The plants began to move in again.

"I will go, green witch, but know that you have made an enemy of the winged goddess this day."

"I think she is already my enemy, but I will keep in mind how not making you a poison might have made her more of an enemy then she is already."

"Sarcasm?"

"You are brilliant. Now leave this place, strange elf, and don't return or it will not be pleasant for you. In fact, if I see you come back, I will have my plants use you as fertilizer."

Tanyth bowed, "As you wish." He eyed her with a gaze that made her blood run cold before he turned and left.

Chapter 9
Dark Mistress

Thessa awoke from deep slumber by the sound of metallic jiggling and whispers. It was subtle, but still fairly noisy. Someone was trying to get into her room by picking the lock under her doorknob.

"You imbeciles." She heard a voice whisper. "Stand aside, did you forget I have the key?"

By the light of the moon pouring in through her window, she searched for the pouch of gold. The whispered voice sounded like the innkeeper. He had eyed her gold. She quickly rushed to the chest of drawers and retrieved the pouch; her slight weight was not enough to make any sound upon the polished wooden floors. She waited in the pallid moonlight as the door creaked open. At the last moment,

Thessa hid the gold pouch under her pillow and pulled the dagger of the Black Mage she still carried from its hiding place.

"Stop, I'm armed." She said as the door revealed the innkeeper and two very large individuals.

"Armed?" The innkeeper held out the lantern before him to reveal Thessa and her dagger. "With a small dagger?" The man looked at each of the two brawny men amusingly then laughed; the two men followed suit.

A fourth man made his way into the room and motioned for the door to be closed. It was the numismatist. "I'll be needing that gold back, miss."

Thessa was surprised but kept her composure. "I am afraid not. You paid me fairly for my coin with it, remember."

"You should have just taken the two gold magi I offered. I would have let those go without incident."

It will happen innocently at first. Something small will set you off and you will be on your way. Sarren's words reverberated in her head. "I.. I sold my coin to you." It was all she could think of saying.

"Well," the numismatist said, "perhaps we could negotiate. I will allow you three gold magi and you return the rest to me now and these fine fellows will leave you the way we have found you," he looked her up and down, "as a pathetic, skinny sot."

"A sot? But I don't drink." Thessa replied.

"Humph, I have seen it before. A sunken-eyed sot selling the family heirlooms for a few gold to buy more drink. You show all the signs. Now, give me what I came for so I can send these men home."

Thessa moved forward with dagger in hand. The men moved back slightly. "Let me keep four."

"I grow wary. I will allow you four if you hand over the rest now."

Thessa reached under her pillow and produced the pouch. She took out three gold magi, one she had already spent on the room and clothes and handed over the gold.

The numismatist weighed out the bag on his hand and then poured some out to look at them. "It seems to all be here." He moved behind the men and opened the door. "Good work, men. She has your gold pieces." With that, he closed the door. The big men brushed aside the dagger she had pointed at them again and pried the gold pieces from her hand. They each took a piece.

"I'll tell Sienna!" Thessa said.

The innkeeper smiled back at her, "You do that. I'm sure she will be most displeased with me. Only, a few silver crowns from this gold magi will speak louder than you, I'm sure of it."

"You won't get away with this!" Thessa said as they exited the room.

"It seems we already have." Came the reply.

Thessa sat on the bed and sighed.

After the door closed, something stirred in the room and Thessa shifted her weight in a startled twitch.

Oh, come now, came a familiar voice, *are you going to just let them walk away?*

Thessa stood up to see the cat Sarren appear at the window. *I see the coin master walking and whistling down the street.*

"You can hear him whistling?"

Well, yes. I can. Are you going to do something? Anything? They just cheated you out of eighty gold magi!

"I heard your evil words as they flooded into my mind while they were here, and I held back. I am resolved not to be the Black Mage! With the tournament coming, Cassany will be forced to bestow it upon someone else. If I hold out long enough, she will run short of training time, and I will be freed."

You stupid simpleton. She will never let you go. You are cursed with this now. The only way out is to die.

A third voice suddenly rang out in a command, "Do it! Be done with it!"

Thessa looked around and then focused on Sarren. She was no longer a cat, but instead a ghostly apparition floating just above the floor. The apparition floated directly to her. The ghostly, ethereal face was pale and terrible. Her eyes were blank.

"Sarren?" Thessa asked cautiously. "No Cassany! Don't do this! Keep Sarren away from me!"

"I obey, goddess." Sarren said, quickly moving faster toward Thessa.

"What are you doing?" Thessa fell back as Sarren entered her body. Thessa reared up and thrashed around, trying to fight the spirit of Sarren taking over her body from the inside. It felt as if she were burning from the inside out. A moment later she was looking at herself in the mirror. Her eyes were a milky white and her fingers were long and twisted. Thessa was along for the ride as Sarren used her usurped hands to open the window and move out into the night. Thessa felt every sensation but could do nothing to stop herself. She felt Sarren in her mind, but consciousness was far away. She could not hear Sarren's thoughts.

"No Sarren, let me go! I don't want you to do this." She screamed into the darkness of her mind. There was no reply.

Thessa was surprised when she felt the back of her hands push off the ground and she began to run on all fours. She could hear herself grunting like some beast. Ahead was the numismatist. She recognized his gait. He turned to the sound of her rushing toward him, and he recoiled. He was not fast enough. Her jagged claws slashed at his throat, and she found herself biting down on his neck. He whimpered rather than screamed. She took the pouch from under his belt. A feeling of satisfaction pervaded her senses. In a moment of clarity, Thessa all at once felt a connection with Sarren. She touched the other's mind. Thessa seized the moment, "No, get out! Thessa cried, and the spirit of Sarren was taken off guard. The ethereal woman exited her body with a jolt. She immediately tried to re-enter, but Thessa blocked her with her dark magic.

The ethereal woman lowered her eyes menacingly, "There you are!" Sarren said. "I knew you were in there somewhere. I knew you would eventually be forced to use your magic."

The magic flowing through Thessa was intoxicating. It made her want to give in to it. It made her thirst for more! "This is what it always feels like?"

"Yes, always. Now, go after the others!" Sarren said. "They have what belongs to you! Get your gold back!"

Even though Thessa wanted to resist, she just couldn't. Her power flowed through her. She suddenly wanted to see what this magic could do. "It feels like trying not to eat the last piece of delicious cheese on the tray, but at the same time knowing you are about to devour it anyway, before anyone else can take it."

"Yes, eat that last piece of cheese, Thessa. Go on, you deserve it. You want it! It's yours!"

"There is no way they will survive!" Thessa said. "I have been so weak! I should not have let them take my property from me."

"No, you shouldn't have, but you are no longer weak, are you!"

"No!"

"With your vengeance on each one of them, this feeling will grow stronger, and you will be more and more elated."

Thessa bounded on all fours toward the inn. With each lope, she felt the wind through her fur. There was no pain, no regret. Each time her hand lifted from the ground, it felt as though she were flying. She could smell the innkeeper. She didn't know how or why, but she knew his scent and she made her way to him. The man was in the alley with the two others who had violated the sanctity of her room. They were laughing, smoking pipes, and drinking wine. She rounded the final corner with the men in sight. The innkeeper saw her, let out a terrified yelp, and headed for a back-alley door. He never made it, Thessa tore out his throat before he had a chance to turn the doorknob.

"What in the two hells *is* that thing?" One of the men shouted. Thessa turned on him, and he was either too stupid or too dumbfounded to move. She dispatched him with animal precision. The final man did make it into the inn either. Thessa followed him, tearing the door from its hinges. Her sharp hearing picked up stirring in the rooms. The guests were waking up from the commotion. Reluctantly, Thessa bounded to her room and lay panting on the floor. She tried to calm herself. She wanted to go back out and rip the man's throat, but she knew she would be caught. She tried to breathe. "How do I shut this off?"

Sarren floated into the room beside her. "You have the magic."

Thessa willed herself to change back, and she did in an instant. All the feelings of what she had done hit her at once, and she both liked it and was disturbed by it. "So, this is how you felt when you murdered Hana's family?"

"Your mother, yeah sure, only, after you do it a few times, it becomes second nature. Now that you have given in to the darkness of the magic, will you once again try to be the good little Thessa?"

"I... I don't know." The adrenaline began to wear off and Thessa's remorse began to settle in and she felt ashamed. "What have I done?"

"There is no use in feeling bad about your new nature, Thessa. Embrace it." The apparition floated up to her face, "The curse is just beginning. Now that you have given in, you will hunger for it. It will consume you, and the craving will get worse the longer you try to live without it. Eventually, it will have its way with you."

Suddenly Thessa became angry, "You forced me! I was going to beat this, and you forced me! You did this against my will! You and Cassany."

"Well, yes. You know, cursed! I told you Cassany would win." Sarren floated back toward the window.

Thessa once again looked at herself in the mirror. Her gaunt face was covered in blood. She used the washbasin and cleaned herself off. "You once used the guise of a man. I can use this dark magic to change the way I look? How exactly does one do that and keep the look for more than just a few hours?"

"Easy, with every kill, you have the power to shift into anything you want."

Thessa gazed into the mirror, "I want to be a beautiful woman, not a girl, a woman, and I want the look to stay with me. The kind every man would desire." She stared into the mirror as her features changed. Her sunken face filled out and her skin became milky smooth. Light streaks accented her dark hair. She turned to get Sarren's appraisal. "Well, what do you think?"

"Beautiful," Sarren replied with a devilish grin, "You are absolutely gorgeous. You have taken your first step. I will warn you. You will be noticed now. Men, and some women, will react differently to you now that you are beautiful."

Thessa willed for Sarren to float to her, and the ghost moved involuntarily.

"What are you doing? Let me go!" Sarren pleaded.

Thessa reached out and took Sarren by the throat. Her hand was able to make purchase on Sarren's ethereal skin. "I bind you to me, Sarren. You will never be able to enter my mind and body like that ever again. I control you." Thessa's new-found magic surged through her into Sarren. "Now, return to being my cat."

"No, I don't want to be a... cat." Immediately, Sarren was the black and white cat again.

Forget the dark magic, you are just as cruel without it! Sarren's voice was once again sounding inside Thessa's mind.

Chapter 10
A Tale of Winter's Chill

Evening approached as Ephaltus relaxed in his favorite chair within the Earth Chamber. The dryads were busy with meal preparations and cleaning while Marlee tended to the cozy fire in the fireplace. He was about to get his pipe out when there was a sharp tapping on the door.

Ephaltus raised up, "Who in the world would knock on a tree? Is the door not under an illusion?" He went to the door of the Earth Chamber and unbolted the carved door. It swung open to reveal a young man with a parchment.

"Oh, yes, did you find the scroll I sent you for." Ephaltus asked happily.

"Yes sir," the boy replied. "It was difficult to smuggle out of the libr..."

"Ah hem, I'll take that." Ephaltus said before the boy could continue his explanation. "Wait here and I will get you what I promised." He returned with a few pieces of silver. "Here is your payment."

The boy checked the silver, "Very generous, sir. Please consider me your man for whatever you need."

"I'll do that." Ephaltus said. The boy smiled and tossed one of the silver pieces up into the air and caught it happily as he turned.

"What is on the parchment?" Marlee asked.

Ephaltus looked up, "Hmm? What were you asking?"

"I asked what you have there."

"Oh, this is a parchment about the distant history of our realm. It's very rare and delicate."

"History? About the tournament?"

"No, it's my retirement project if you must know. I am looking deep into the history of the realm. When you are Tourney Master, I plan to spend my remaining days looking onto the past. I may even write a few scrolls of parchment about it myself."

"What a wonderful idea." Marlee said. "I'll look forward to reading them."

"Um, yes, well, I have a room in the Arsenal of the Way I'm using to store my work safely. I think I will go and find a place for this if you will be satisfied with your work here?"

"Certainly, go on. I don't need you hovering over me while I study the book of rules you gave me."

"It's not a book of rules." Ephaltus corrected.

"It talks a lot about decorum. Seems very much like rules to me."

"It's advice. What to look for and how to keep the mages and their gods on the straight and narrow."

"Yes, rules."

Ephaltus huffed, "I will be in the Arsenal should you need me."

"Mm hm," Marlee answered.

Ephaltus left the Earth Chamber and made his way to the Arsenal of the Way, all the while huffing and puffing at how troubling Marlee could be when she insisted on going against him. He went to the back wall of the arsenal and looked around nervously. When he was satisfied no one had followed him and that there were no prying eyes or Ocularius lens focused on him, he held out his hand and focused his fingers in a horn pattern with the two middle fingers of his right hand lowered toward his palm while the outer two fingers pointed strait up.

"Elesence Eliptus," he said. The weapons rack before him faded into a portal about the size of a door one might use with a closet. Not too wide or tall as to give room for larger creatures to pass. He entered the room beyond, and the portal closed. The room was vast and filled with treasures. To his left another row of books went as far as one could see in the dim torchlight. To his left shelves with dusty trinkets lined the walls until they too disappeared into the darkness. Hanging from the ceiling were nets filled with other, larger lightweight treasures such as wooden crates with more papers and materials. He took one of the torches and lit it from one of the sconces and proceeded down the dusty thoroughfare. After a short time, he came to a great wooden desk covered in parchment and trinkets. He held his hand up again and spoke a few more cryptic words. The dust swirled from the desk and crackled into nothingness in heatless sparkles.

"Who goes there?" An ominous voice boomed from somewhere deeper inside.

"It is I, Shelayla. No need to be concerned." Ephaltus said. "No need to get up on my account."

"You have not been here for quite some time, wizard. How do I know you are who you say you are?"

"Don't be daft."

"Ah, That's it. Welcome, Ephaltus." A scaly head appeared from the darkness, a head with horns and a long snout and mouth filled with sharp teeth. Shelayla was a dragon scarcely larger than a normal horse. "What trinket have you brought for me to guard?"

Ephaltus opened the scroll. "Sometimes I think you believe this is your treasure to hoard."

"Most of it is."

"Well, I didn't bring you any gold or whatnot. This time it is knowledge, knowledge of the past on this scroll."

"Oh, and what have you discovered?"

Ephaltus read the scroll for a few moments. "I was right, Shelayla. This scroll is a piece torn from scrolls of creation. It tells of a seventh god! Behold the great god Cryonias whose frozen core chills the world. Behold and harken to the Tale of Winter's Chill. It's a story related to the seventh god. I can barely contain my elation!"

"It sounds like a made-up children's story." Shelayla said. "What makes you think it's anything but an old tale to entertain children and simpletons?"

"That's what I intend to find out. This is not the only reference to the seventh god. I do need more evidence if I intend to prove another god exists or existed." He grinned dreamily, "Wouldn't it be something if I could locate the seventh god? I would be known for more than simply an old Tourney Master. If I did discover the seventh god and expose the other six gods, that would show those pompous deities. I might even be able to achieve my dream of ending the Tournament of Mages forever."

"Oh, so, that is what the other gods will think of this endeavor? That you bested them somehow? They will just stop the tournament at your behest?"

"I hope so."

"Perhaps they will welcome your discovery. Maybe they had nothing to do with the disappearance of the seventh god and will thank you for his return."

Ephaltus furrowed his brow, "I had not thought about that. I just assumed they all were up to something nefarious. I suppose I don't really care what they think."

"Okay, so let us explore the opposite. What if they killed or exiled the seventh god, as you assume? Won't they be upset with you for digging up the evidence and try to stop or destroy you?"

"Are you asking if one of them might interfere with my investigation or threaten me in some way?"

"I suppose I am."

"I say that would have to be some seriously strong evidence."

"Does it tell you where to look?"

Ephaltus studied the scroll, "I think it does, but it's in a riddle, of course. I suppose the starting location to begin finding an exiled god would not be obvious. I'll have to figure it all out while I'm in this hidden chamber. There are too many eyes on the Arsenal of the Way and the Earth Chamber." He cleared a spot on his desk and laid out the scroll. He sat and began to decode the cryptic text. Shelayla, knowing not to disturb him when he was working, resumed her task of protecting the hidden treasures of the Arsenal of the Way.

"Hmm, this is partially written in the language of the ancient Southlanders. Maybe the place I need to find the next clue is in one of the ruins of the Broken Lands," he said. He looked up and Shelayla was gone. "Hmm, when did she leave?" He shrugged to himself and returned to his task.

A few moments later, Shelayla returned. "I may have something for you. When I was searching for food in the Broken Lands, I found something in the ruins of Jenti on the north island." She placed a small statue of a bird on his desk.

"What's this?" Ephaltus asked.

"Use arcane magic on it."

Ephaltus willed his arcane magic on the statue. It began to animate and speak. "Seek out the Raven for the breath of winter and to hear the Tale of Winter's Chill. Beware the Raven if your intentions are insincere." It kept repeating the same message until Ephaltus stopped it.

"Did you hear me say I thought the clue to this mystery was in the Broken Lands? I thought you had wondered off."

"I did not hear you say anything about the Broken Lands, but I did notice the upper right-hand corner of your scroll." Ephaltus glanced back at the scroll in the upper right-hand corner. There was a small image of a raven in the exact likeness of the small statue.

"Ah, ha, So, I was right. The next clue is in the Broken lands. Thank you, Shelayla, you have given me confirmation of where I need to go next. As usual you are invaluable to me."

Shelayla grinned, "I live to find treasure; it's in my blood."

"Indeed, Now I must prepare to travel. I wonder if Marlee is ready to handle things here on her own for a time?"

"The mages are training at the moment, right?"

"They have only barely begun. Most of them are still unaware of their power."

"Perfect! Marlee really has nothing to do but watch over them. It is the perfect time for you to travel to the Broken lands."

Ephaltus cupped his chin and tapped absently with his forefinger, "Yes, you're right. As long as I can get her to remember to calibrate the Ocularius Magnus on a regular basis, I think she will be fine here on her own for a mere couple of weeks."

"She will be fine."

Ephaltus was amused at the dragon's enthusiasm. "You are just as curious as I am, aren't you?"

"Well, yes. A seventh god few have ever heard of before! A monumental mystery, as timely as the world itself. It is very exciting. I want to see you succeed and find out what happened."

"I will find out, Shelayla, I will. I promise you!"

Chapter 11
The Young Man in the Marketplace

Thessa kept to the shadows most of the time until she realized her disguised face made her blend in with the locals quite nicely. She was no longer the pasty-faced girl with gaunt cheeks and sunken eyes. She no longer had the appearance of a reformed blood feeder. She was surprised each and every time a lady or gentleman acknowledged her with a grin, smile, or tip of the hat. She was so used to passers-by going out of their way to ignore her or avoid eye contact.

Thessa set her destination to the marketplace at the edge of the town square. Sarren, as a cat, remained in her room at the Suckling Pig Inn. The encounter she had with the numismatist and his henchmen persuaded her to hold off on finding out where her treasure from Cassany was hidden. The coins she had on her would suffice for quite some time before she had to squeeze the information out of Sarren.

In the meantime, she needed some fruit and other foodstuff for the room. Even looking as fetching as she was now, she wanted to avoid going down into the common room as much as possible. She planned to see if she could appeal to the innkeeper to hire a kitchen maid to bring her meals, but she had not gathered the courage yet.

Since she had arrived in the big city, her experience told her she could not trust anyone. She decided to avoid interactions with people as much as she could. She entered the marketplace clutching her coin purse. She was not about to let some random cutpurse get away with snatching it from her after the price she paid to secure them. The marketplace was a long street on the sunny side of the city where the walls were lower, yet still heavily guarded by the Emlestra city militia. The first section she came to was the produce quarter. Rows and rows of apples, pears, corn ears, tomatoes, and other fruits and vegetables were displayed on slanting, open carts and shelves. Further down the street were the cloth merchants and dry good sellers. She began at the apple and pear cart, replaying the exchange of currency in her head so she would not be cheated.

She was not far into her shopping before she noticed a man following her from cart to cart. Her first instinct was to panic. After what had happened to her at the inn, she had become more and more paranoid. She moved to the next cart a little faster than before and she nonchalantly glanced around but did not see the man. She breathed in a sigh of relief. She cautiously began rummaging through the fruit and vegetables once again.

"Excuse me?"

Thessa was startled to hear the sound of a man's voice right behind her. She turned quickly to see the man who was following her stand-in right next to her. She let out a little yelp then covered her mouth.

"I'm so sorry." He said, "I didn't mean to startle you. It's just that you look so familiar. I had also hoped to get your help on picking out some of this fruit. I don't know how to tell if it's too ripe."

"Sneaking up on a girl probably isn't the best way to go about asking." Thessa said.

The man lowered his head, "You're right. I am such an idiot."

"Oh, no. I didn't mean for you to feel bad about yourself. I was just saying..."

"It is difficult to build up the courage to talk to someone as lovely as you." He grimaced, "Wow, that sounded better in my head."

Thessa didn't know what to say, so she just stood there awkwardly.

"I'm sorry." He reached out with his hand, "Name's Gaelyn." Thessa took his hand.

"I'm called Thessa."

"Thessa, that's a nice name." He kissed the top of her hand.

"I'm sure you would say that even if it wasn't."

"You know, I probably would." They both chuckled.

Thessa looked deep into Gaelyn's eyes before concluding he was genuinely friendly and didn't have something else in mind. He had forgotten that she looked different from normal for a few moments, and she briefly wondered if he might be talking to her because she was beautiful. Would he have given her any notice had she still looked like herself?

"I know this is sudden, but would you consider a meal with me this evening?" Gaelyn was distracted by the mewing of a black and white cat that had just shown up and began rubbing Thessa's leg. "Oh, who is this little fellow?"

"*She* is my cat, Sarren, and she was supposed to be in our room at the inn. How did you get out?"

The maid

"Bad kitty!"

"That is amazing. How did she find you out here?"

"She is a very smart animal."

"I should say so. You can bring her along if you consent to have a meal with me this evening."

"I would love to."

Bad idea. You are forgetting yourself. If you develop feelings for this man, you will be putting him in grave danger.

"It's only dinner."

Gaelyn flinched, "Okay, only dinner and we will see how it goes from there."

"Oh no, I was speaking to my cat. I... uh... do that sometimes. I think she came to find me because she's hungry."

"Oh." He looked confused.

Thessa tried to reassure him, "My cat and I have a special bond. It's like I can read her thoughts sometimes. Don't put too much into it. I am just crazy about my kitty. I hope that isn't a problem for you?"

"No, not at all. I like cats." He bent down to pet her, and Sarren hissed and pawed at him. He jerked his hand away.

"Sarren, no! Bad kitty." She bent down and picked her up. "You stop that!"

Well, he needs to go away.

"I think you had better go back to our rooms." She indicated a booth across the street with a fat man eyeing them hungrily. There were dead cats hanging from the ceiling in the shop and along the outer eve. "I think some around these parts must eat cats." Sarren eyed the man with horror.

Gaelyn looked at the booth, "Oh yes, I had forgotten about them. There is another booth down the way where they sell dogs for dinner as well. Barbaric!"

Thessa let Sarren go and she ran in the opposite direction, out of sight.

"Will she be all right by herself?" Gaelyn asked.

"She will. She is stronger than you know. Stronger than the average house cat."

"And smarter too."

Thessa chuckled, "Yes, and smarter too."

"I know it is still a while until dinnertime, but how about we walk the market together? We can decide on where and what to eat as we go."

"I'd like that." Thessa said. She was glad to have company in such a dangerous place, and Gaelyn didn't seem like a danger to her in any way. Besides, if he tried anything, he would surely be surprised to find she could defend herself in ways he would immediately regret. They strolled down the market, stopping at shops and booths to try on scarves and whatnots. She was having a grand time. No one had ever paid attention to her like this before. About an hour into the walk, several men began to run from their booths. She heard someone from one of the booths tell his son to mind the shop. He had to run to the cat booth because Jerron was being attacked and maimed by a vicious black and white cat.

Gaelyn looked with surprise at Thessa, "You don't think?"

"No, I'm sure it's not my cat."

"We had better check for sure. Maybe he got a hold of her."

"All right, but I'm telling you it wasn't her."

They hurriedly returned to the cat booth. It didn't take long to reach it since they were not stopping at each booth along the way. When they got to the booth, the cats were no longer hanging from the ceiling and eve and the man, Jerron, was hunched over the counter with his face in ruins and his cloths all covered in his own blood. Thessa knew immediately that Sarren had indeed killed the man. Whether he had hunted her down or she had returned just to do the job was unclear. She knew she could not let this stand, so she went to the man.

"Is he dead?" A woman standing by asked.

"As dead as can be." Said one of the men.

Thessa went to him and held his hand, "I don't think he's dead," she said. "Here, help me get him on this table inside the booth. Someone get some water and cloth and clean his wounds."

"I'll be right back." Said the woman as she ran to the nearby water well after stopping at her booth for some strips of cloth.

Thessa knew the man was dead, but she pretended he was breathing. "See his chest moves."

"I don't see it." The nosey man said, craning his head to get a better look.

"Well, he is breathing. I can see his chest move."

"She speaks the truth." Gaelyn said.

Thessa thought it was kind of him to back her up, even though she knew he couldn't see the chest movement either.

The woman returned with the water and cloth and began cleaning Jerron's face. Thessa concentrated and tried her best not to show what she was doing as she healed the deep cuts on the man's face. His face would be scarred, but at least he would not start hemorrhaging when she raised him. She placed her hand on his chest and let her energy flow into him. "See, he lives."

The man suddenly sat upright, "Where is that damned cat?" Was his first words.

"Sssh, it's gone now. Lie back down. You are still hurt." Thessa said, making him lie back on the table.

"I guess you were right, miss. I thought for sure her was a goner." The nosey man said.

"No flipping cat will do me in, friend!" Jerron yelled out to him.

"You will be fine, now." Thessa said. She returned to Gaelyn, who was still in front of the booth. "I am covered in blood. I need to go back to my inn room and wash up."

"That was amazing. Are you a healer?" Gaelyn asked.

"No, but I knew a nanny who took care of three children. I learned a few things here and there from her."

"Let us get you to your inn hero of the market," Gaelyn said. "Afterward we can go for a proper outing."

Thessa looked around and all the people were smiling at her and nodding at her with their appreciation and approval. "I can manage. Why don't I meet you somewhere in say... about an hour?"

"All right. Why don't you just meet me here in the market?" He pointed to a booth selling flowers. "At the flower booth there."

"I will see you in an hour at the flower cart then, " Thessa said. She hurriedly moved away from him.

"I will wait for you!" Gaelyn called after her.

Chapter 12
Before Dawn

J as poured the ale and slammed it down on the counter, causing some of it to spill out on his patron. "Oy, Jas, you big oaf, careful with me ale!"

"Drink it up, Cedric, before I call in that tab of yours." Jas threatened.

The big man behind the counter went to pour another mug of ale when the door to the tavern suddenly burst open. Snowy wind blew in and two men sitting close to the opening rushed to close the door behind the man who stumbled in. He looked at the bartender and let down his hand from the wound on his neck and it began gushing blood.

"He's killed us all! Lock the door. He is coming! Lock the door!" The man collapsed onto the tavern floor.

Jas came from behind the counter with a bottle of hard liquor. He pushed two tables together. "Here men, get him up here." They lifted the man onto the tables. "Where is Jon the barber?"

"Here!" Jon responded from somewhere near the rear of the tavern. He rushed up to the wounded man.

"Here's some hard mash. What else do you need to help this poor fellow?"

"Bandages." The barber replied.

The injured man stirred and grabbed the barber by his shirt, "You don't understand. He's coming!"

"Who's coming, friend?" Jas asked.

The door creaked open, letting more snowy wind blow in. A shadowy figure entered the common room of the inn. The men once again rushed to close the door.

"No! He's here. Run!"

The light of the lantern near the door still swung back and forth from the wind blowing inside, illuminating the face of the man, and then swinging in the other direction, leaving it in darkness.

"Who are you, friend?"

The man on the table whispered, "We're all dead. He's here. Sir Danton has killed us."

The light of the lantern swung back to shine on the stranger's face. He was smiling now with a toothy grin, exposing four long sharp canine teeth, still partially drenched in blood.

∞

Night was falling over the mountains as Tanyth Veridian rode his horse through the moderately deep snow. When he reached the other side of the mountain pass, he could see the inn in the distance. As he drew closer to the place, he could feel the cold embrace of death upon it. A thick white smoke bellowed from its two chimneys, each located on both ends of the building. Whatever death he was sensing must not have occurred long ago. He made his way to the front of the inn and tied his horse to the hitching post most protected from the weather under the eaves of the wrap-around porch roof. The front door was open, and he pushed it all the way open with ease. He stepped into the common room and closed the door behind him. The room was warm and well-lit despite the cold air that must have been blowing in. The sconces and braziers were still burning, and the two fireplaces contained roaring fires. Lying across the bar from back to front was a big man with blood dripping from a neck wound, He was obviously the innkeeper by the looks of his white apron. The broken bottle clutched in his right hand said that he had tried to fight off his attacker. Tanyth visited the first table closest to the door and pulled back one of the dead by grasping a tuft of his hair. The man's eyes were opened and fixed in a gaze of terror.

"Well, you are no good to ask." Tanyth said as he let the man fall back to his death position. Several of the men in the place laid strewn about, and one was flat on the floor not far from the entrance, but he kept finding himself returning to the innkeeper. He decided he would try him. He made his way through the dead to the innkeeper and raised his head. The wound on his neck stopped trickling for a moment. The man's expression was not nearly as terrified as the first man. "You'll do." Tanyth grasped the man's head and let his energy flow. The innkeeper lurched and coughed. He sputtered back away from Tanyth.

"Who in the two hells are you?" He looked around frantically, brandishing his broken bottle. "What happened? Where is that vampire?"

"So, there was a blood feeder here? Since you are looking for him, I don't suppose you would know where he was headed next. Seems I have wasted my time and energy. If you know anything useful to me, then speak."

The innkeeper stiffened a bit, "they said his name was Sir Danton. From the armor he wore, I would say he was one of the king's kin."

"Ah, so you do have some useful information after all."

"He was so quick. I tried to stop him, but he was so quick."

"Was that everything you know of him?"

"I thought blood feeders were a thing of the past. How is it he came into being?"

"That's all, I guess. Go back to your slumber." The innkeeper fell dead again immediately back onto the counter.

Tanyth looked around and then hesitated a moment. "I hate to let all these good men go to waste. I should bring you all back from the realm of the dead to serve me, but I am afraid that would be a conflict with the dark one Cassany is training, a pity." He went behind the counter, took out his blade and severed the left hand of the innkeeper. Then he reached behind the counter onto the liquor shelf and took two full clear bottles. He sniffed them to make sure they were the proof he needed, and then he emptied the contents on the floor, being sure to splash some of it over the dead. He backed his way to the entrance and tossed the empties into the inn. With a snap of his fingers, he ignited a spark which landed in one of the pools of alcohol. The fire spread quickly and soon engulfed the inn.

"Show me the way," he said to the severed hand, which burst into life at his touch. He dropped the hand onto the ground, and it ran off, running on the fingertips like a demented spider. "Slowly now." Tanyth called after it and the hand slowed down. Tanyth crawled into his saddle after releasing his horse from the hitching post and pulled the reins for the horse to follow the hand. The beast let out a grunt that ended with a jet of smoke and flame from its nostrils. Its dead eyes fixed on the severed hand and Tanyth Veridian was off after the blood feeder. As he rode away from the inn, he left the place behind him completely engulfed in flames as large plumes of grey smoke rose into the cold winter air.

CHAPTER 13

Reunion

Thessa hurried back to the inn and into her room where Sarren was sitting in the window licking the blood off her fur. "What did you do?" Thessa asked.

He had to die. What a barbarian!

"You have put us both in danger. People saw you. If you come out of here with me again, someone will recognize you." Thessa began to strip the bloody clothes and wash.

Wait, why do you have blood on you?

"I brought the man back."

Why would you do such a thing? I must go back.

"You will stay put here in this room. I did it so you would not be hunted down and killed. Now, you are just dangerous."

She gazed at the white in Sarren's fur, "I wonder." She reached down and touched the white fur and commanded it to true black. The fur changed. "Hmm, there you go. All black now. No, now saw a fully black cat attacking a man in the market." She went back to cleaning the blood. "No more killing people unless you clear it through me first."

But you will never say yes!

"Now you are understanding. No, I will not."

Some black mage I am training you to be. Cassany will not stand for this. She will make you a killer whether you like it or not.

"I have no doubt she will try."

I have no doubt she will succeed.

Thessa glared at her but kept washing, and then she went to get some fresh clothing.

You are not going back out there to meet that man, are you?

"That is of no consequence to you, servant."

You are going to get him killed or worse.

"Shut up, you stupid cat. I am the Black Mage, remember. I know what I'm doing. Besides, it's just a meal. I am not going off to marry him or something."

That is how it all starts. You have been hideous all this time and now that you have looks and you're getting attention, you are running off to the first man who said you were pretty.

"I wasn't hideous."

You were a gaunt, hideous blood feeder.

"I was getting my strength back after my mother cured me of it. I would have eventually recovered. I have no doubt I will recover even now." She finished dressing. "You are to stay here. Only come if I call you to me. If you disobey me, I will make sure you never do again."

Oh, what will you do? Turn me into something else, spank me, yell at me? I know you will talk me to death with kind words and a smile.

"You have not seen my dark side. It's there. I vowed never to let it surface again once I was cured. I might just let it come back for a good cause, like punishing you!" She exited the room and came face to face with Hana, her mother and Red Mage. She froze. Hana smiled at her and walked around her.

"Excuse me." She said as she passed. Thessa stepped aside. She turned to watch Hana stroll down the hall. She was flooded with a myriad of emotions. Hana stood there in the corridor searching for the room she had rented from downstairs. She looked at Thessa with a kind smile, and Thessa's knees went weak.

"Excuse me, miss. Is this the way to room seven?" Hana asked.

Thessa did not comprehend the question at first and she stood there unmoving and silent.

"Miss, are you all right?"

"Hmm? Yes, sorry. What was it you were asking me?"

"I am so sorry to bother you. But this inn is arranged strangely, and I was wondering if this corridor might contain the door to room seven."

"Yes, this room here is my room, room six. Your room is the door there across from mine. The numbers on these doors are faded and painted over in black, but if you look closely, you can see it still in the dark impression of the door."

"Thank you, kindly." Hana said. Thessa moved past her in the corridor and picked up the pace to get away. She had to process this new development. "Um, excuse me. I hate to bother you again."

Thessa turned at the end of the corridor just above the stairwell to acknowledge her, "Yes?"

"You seem familiar. Have we met before?"

"I was thinking the same thing." Thessa lied. "Was it possible her mother could see her even through this facade? We must have run into each other somewhere."

"What is your name, dear?"

"My name?" Thessa suddenly froze again. "What was she going to tell her?"

"Yes, dear. You have a name, don't you?"

"Yes, it's... Zarina." She had a friend named Zarina when she was young. It was the only name she could think of on the spur of the moment.

"That's a lovely name." Hana said. "I knew a Zarina when I was younger. She used to hang around the house when..." Her face suddenly became ashen and sad. "Do you have children?"

"Me? No, I don't." Thessa said, remembering her guise made her appear close to her mother's age.

"I do. I am looking for her now." She squinted at Thessa. "Strange, I am usually tight lipped but I seem to be rambling on with you, forgive me. Thank you for your service." She genuflected slightly.

"Did you find the room?" Came a booming male voice. "Oh, excuse me." The man in a grey cloak said as he met Thessa at the top of the stairs.

"It's not a problem." Thessa said, moving out of his way. Asleth, the Grey Mage, squeezed past her carrying two cloth bags.

"Yes, this is Zarina. She pointed me in the right direction."

"Excellent. Thank you." Asleth said.

"Well, I best be going." Thessa blurted out.

"Oh, nice to meet you." Asleth called after her.

"You as well." Thessa called back as she hastily descended the stairs. She stopped at the bottom and wiped away a tear. She knew her mother would find her eventually, but she thought it would be better if she didn't. It hurt her heart to think Hana blamed herself for Thessa becoming a blood feeder and then worse, the Black Mage, so she thought it might be better for everyone involved if she did not reveal herself. If she was to become the Black Mage against her will, much like Sarren taking matters into her own hands, she couldn't live with herself if she hurt her mother more. It was odd to her that Asleth was still with her. What was his plan? Thessa vowed she would have to find out how to protect her mother. Asleth was known as the protector, but why, and what did it have to do with Hana? She took a deep breath and continued out of the inn and toward the marketplace.

Thessa tried her best not to appear distraught when she met Gaelyn in the marketplace. She spotted him before he spotted her, and she stopped for a moment to look at him carefully. He had sandy brown hair and a warm smile, which we used the moment he saw her. She strolled up to him as if she didn't have a care in the world.

"I was about to think you were not coming," he said.

"I got hung up at the inn. I had to help a nice couple find their room."

"It's okay. It gave me time to plan where I wanted to take you for that meal." He held out his hand and Thessa took it. He led her around the cat man stand. It was closed now and boarded up. But, as they strolled down the marketplace, people recognized her and gave her a big, approving smile or a wave. She cringed at the attention, especially since she found the man and what he was selling repulsive. Still, there was part of her that enjoyed the spotlight for a change. She didn't feel as though everything she did was a mistake or an ill-timed blunder.

"Here we are." Gaelyn pointed to a small booth with four wooden tables arranged in front of it. "They say this place has wonderful food."

"It isn't cat or rat or dog, is it?"

Gaelyn looked quizzical, "I don't think so."

"Or any other disgusting food from under a rock or up a tree or something."

"I guess we will find out. What is it you like?"

"Right now, vegetables!"

Gaelyn laughed and led her to the booth where a man in a food-stained apron was stirring a pot of something.

"May I help you?" The man asked.

"What is your best meal?" Gaelyn asked.

"No, no, no, friend." The man began. "Let me take care of you two fine young people. You cannot walk up to a booth on this marketplace and ask what the best meal is. They will give you whatever concoction they are trying to get rid of before it goes bad. You ask what their freshest meal is." He winked at Thessa, "And they will probably give you whatever is about to go bad, anyway." He laughed uproariously.

"What will you be eating from your place tonight?" Thessa asked.

"Ah, now this is a smart one. You had better hold on to this one. I have a specialty that I like to enjoy. I take two slices of bread and put between them roasted chicken, crispy bacon, and aged cheese and then I bake it in the oven for a few minutes until the cheese melts. I call it a chicken bake."

"Oh, I'll have one of those." Thessa said.

"Make it two." Gaelyn interjected.

"Coming right up. I will make it three! One for me, you know. Sit, sit, and I will serve you with some nice wine to go with your food."

They picked a table and sat. "What a nice fellow." Gaelyn said.

A few more people arrived and the man behind the booth served them the stew he was staring. At least Thessa imagined it was stew. The man winked at her when ladling it into bowls.

"Tell me about yourself." Gaelyn asked her.

She knew he was trying to start a conversation, but he was treading in an area she didn't want to go. "Oh no, you don't. Tell me about yourself first."

"All right. I am a dockworker here in Emlestra. It doesn't pay a lot, and it's hard on my hands, but it's steady work."

"That explains your muscles." She blurted out and then immediately blushed afterward.

Gaelyn fixed his arm muscle, "You think so, huh? Well, I am scrawny compared to some men who work there."

"Here is your food and wine," The booth owner said as he placed two wooden plates before them with the chicken bake on them, and a bottle of wine with two glasses. Gaelyn paid the man, and he walked away satisfied.

"This looks delicious." Thessa observed.

"It does." Gaelyn agreed.

They were halfway through their meal when Hana and Asleth arrived at the booth. The man gave them the same treatment he gave Thessa and Gaelyn, and they turned to find a seat.

Hana spotted Thessa. "Hello again. Small world isn't it."

"Yes, it is." Thessa said. "Gaelyn, this is the woman I helped find her room earlier."

"Oh, so you are the reason she was late." He stood and kissed Hana's hand.

"I was. I am so sorry."

"He is attempting a joke, miss," Thessa said.

"Absolutely, I meant nothing by it."

"Oh, good. You two are such a nice-looking couple. Is the food good here?" Hana asked.

"It's depends on what you ordered," Gaelyn said.

"We were talked into something called a chicken bake."

"Good, that's what we're having. It's delicious." Thessa assured her. She noticed Asleth said nothing and stared at her intently.

"Do I have something in my teeth?" Thessa asked him.

"Hmm? Oh sorry, you just seem so familiar. I am certain we have met before." Asleth said.

"I guess I have one of those faces." Thessa said squiring in her seat. She was thankful when the man brought them their food and their focus was taken off her. She hurried through the meal and then beckoned Gaelyn for them to leave. He got the hint. They said their goodbyes and exchanged a few other pleasantries and left. Gaelyn never questioned her about why she wanted to leave so badly, and she thought that was one of his best qualities.

Chapter 14
Daggers of the Soul

Tanyth Veridian rode his death steed to a farmstead just east of the city of Tama, at the source of the river Taman. By using the severed hand of the fiend's victim, he had traced the vampire the Black Mage had created to the main farmhouse. He dismounted and instructed his horse to stand ready in case the blood feeder was present and inclined to flee. Upon entering the house through a door that had obviously been forced, he was greeted with the first victim, a woman of middle age on the floor lying in a pool of blood.

"Sloppy work," Tanyth said. "You are letting too much of the precious blood go to waste." He heard a grunting noise, and a mischievous smile graced his lips. "So, you *are* still here, good."

There came a sharp squeal from the other room as the fiend heard Tanyth speak. An abrupt burst of footfalls ensued. The thing was fast. It rounded the corner through the doorway with lightning speed. Tanyth employed his magic over death, and the vampire's face twisted in shock as it slowed to a snail's pace. Tanyth held out his hand and grasped Sir Danton by the neck as he slowly tried to skid to a stop. He released his magic and Danton sped immediately back to pace, smacking Tanyth's hand, ensuring his death grip.

"Hello, Sir Danton, I presume?" Danton let out a wounded howl. "Oh, so much anger. A new blood feeder who doesn't know what he is or why he is so ravenous for human flesh. Let me enlighten you. The Black Mage in her current ignorant state created you and then abandoned you to this life. You are now drawn to her like a moth to flame, but you can't help stopping here and there to feed. You need to satiate that horrible hunger after all. She is south of Emlestra. If you are planning on taking the river, don't. The water can be deadly to you. Besides, I have another task for you before you make your presence known to the Black Mage."

"What are you? Are you like me?" Sir Danton's voice was scratchy and harsh.

"No, not exactly. I am not a vampire. I am... something else."

"You are an elf."

"No, I am not exactly an elf either. What I was in the past is no more. It's best we don't get too friendly. Suffice it to say, I do not fear the dead or the undead."

"I must get to the Black Mage."

"Oh, I will fix that." He pressed on Danton's forehead with his free hand. "There, better?"

"I am free from her grasp!" His body went limp in Tanyth's hand.

"Well, for now. I wouldn't get used to it if I were you, but for this moment in time you *are* free of her and under my power. You work for me as long as I am nearby. You will not feel the pull from your creator."

Tanyth peered into the room where Danton had emerged with the blood feeder still clutched in his grasp. A man, presumably the farmer, lay dead straddled over a wooden rocking chair. Tanyth let the fiend go and he stayed at bay. "I must teach you how to feed. You are far too sloppy. At least you have the wits to stay away from villages, towns, and cities where your presence would be felt by the locals."

"My father?"

"You best forget about him. You are far too dangerous to him now. He will send soldiers out to find what happened to you, but soon you will become unrecognizable to him. Blood feeder's features tend to change unless you manage to keep feeding on a regular basis. Even then, your features will distort. Your father is the current king, is he not?"

"Yes, he is the king."

"He is soon to be replaced. You have failed to secure his line." Tanyth breathed in and then grinned maniacally, letting his breath slowly out through his nose. "However, your service to him is not yet done. Once you and I complete our goddess' given task, you shall have made your father proud. Come now, we have a long way to go, and we need to get you a steed."

"Horses shy away from me. I can't get near them." Danton rasped.

"Live ones do." Tanyth said. "We will take care of that, don't worry. Come, let us visit the barn."

∽

Once back in her room at the inn, Thessa felt a pang of dread in her forehead, as if something hard and small had struck her square in the middle of it. She rubbed the offending spot, and the pain subsided. "What the heck was that."

What did you say? Sarren asked telepathically.

"Nothing, I just felt like I got pelted in the forehead with a pebble or small rock for a second."

Oh, that's not good. As far as I know, you have not created any minions, right?

"Never, I would not do to anyone what you did to me. I don't care how much pressure Cassany applies to me."

The pain you describe sounds like what happens when one of the Black Mage minion's link is severed. You are bound to all creatures you create.

"But, as we have established, that can't be it since I have not created any minions as you put it."

Then it could be random body pain. It could mean nothing.

"I'll let you know if I feel it again." Thessa said. "I'm going to change the subject now, and I want you to listen carefully. Do not talk to me in my head when we meet with Gaelyn. I don't want you distracting me."

I will try. Why don't you speak to me in the same way I speak to you?

"Because I don't know how, and I would rather just say it." She stopped and rubbed the spot on her forehead again. "Ouch! There it is again."

Are you certain you have not raised anyone from the dead or created a blood feeder?

"Raise from the dead? That will create a blood feeder?"

Yes. It could if you don't know what you're doing.

"I raised Sir Danton. You were there, remember?"

Yes, but I didn't notice anything unusual. He got up and ran as I remember. That's a common reaction for a human. He was also not dead long enough. The newly dead tend to come back unscathed.

"Well, he was the only one."

What about the man in the market?

"Oh, I had almost forgotten I raised him. He was newly dead too. Could I have made a blood feeder out of him?"

I could never make one until the body had been expired for at least a day. When I tried it on people who had just died, they would rise and live like normal.

"Well, are you a blood feeder? Remember, I raised you too. Shouldn't you be one, I mean?"

Technically, yes! Cassany said she stopped the process so I could instruct you.

"When did you talk to Cassany?"

The same time you did, remember?

Thessa took a deep breath. "I have something else to tell you. My mother and Asleth are here."

In the city?

"In this inn, staying right across the hall. They also came to the same food booth Gaelyn took me to. It was awkward. Asleth almost figured out who I was."

How? You look completely different.

"They kept saying how I looked familiar to them."

Maybe they are just passing through and will be gone tomorrow. They have no reason to believe you are here, do they?

"We can hope. I don't plan to reveal who I am to them."

I thought as much. Why would you?

"It would just cause more harm than good. Look at what has happened already!" She glanced out the window. "I know she blames herself for you turning me into a blood feeder and then my foolish stunt leading to me being who I am now, which is also your fault!"

You think I wanted to serve my killer as a feline? I didn't plan this.

"Something is going on with me, Sarren, and I need to know what. I have released something into the world I need to find it and remove it. I need your help. How do I track these things and kill them?"

Tracking them is easy. You are the Black Mage, and you can sense the dead and undead. Killing them is also easy. You just will them dead but...

"But what?"

They are kind of like your children. When you are close to them, you will not want to destroy them. You will need to be strong, stronger than you have ever been before, or you will not be able to bring yourself to do it. It will be like stabbing your own soul to kill them.

"If they are blood feeders, I will be able to. I remember what it's like. I would have rather been dead than do the things I was forced to do just to survive. I hated every minute of it."

I hope so because I am telling you right now. It will be the most soul wrenching thing you can do.

"No, I have already done the most soul wrenching thing I could do."

I don't think you have. I do believe you think you have, but you have not, not yet.

Thessa changed the subject, "So, what is the first thing I need to do to track these things?"

There is nothing to it. You just concentrate and think about them, and you will see them. You might want to lie down and meditate first to clear your head of everything so you can see them clearly.

Thessa prepared for bed and then laid flat on her back. She cleared her mind and thought about any blood feeders she may have created. "Wait, what happened to the blood feeders you created?"

If they are still out there, you will not be able to detect them. They were mine, not yours. When vampires invade a town without someone to lead them looking for blood, they usually don't last long as you probably already know.

Thessa retrained her thoughts on the task at hand; she let her mind wander and suddenly she could see them. "Oh no! I see them and something is wrong, Sarren. I see about ten of them. I know I didn't resurrect that many people. What in the two hells? What does this mean?"

It means Sir Danton is a Sanquinator. We need to find him as soon as we can or there will be a lot more soon.

"A Sanquinator? Is that some kind of super vampire? I have never heard of it before."

That's because I never made one. When you were a vampire, you had no reason to run into one of them. But I know of them from the Black Mage before me.

Thessa bolted upright, "Cassany tricked me! I knew she would! She sent me to raise Danton. She said it was to help my allies. She wanted me to create this abomination."

I hate to say it, but I told you she would have her way with you one way or another.

Thessa fumed, "Come morning, we will make a plan to intercept and stop this."

What about Gaelyn?

Thessa sighed, "I don't have time for Gaelyn. He will just have to understand."

Chapter 15
The Broken Lands

When Ephaltus returned to the Earth Chamber, Marlee was talking to one of the dryads about redecorating. He heard a snippet of the conversation as he was putting up his cloak. "What is all this about?" he asked as he moved to where Marlee and the dryad talked.

"This place needs a woman's touch." Marlee said. "You don't expect me to live here like this, do you?"

"Like what?"

"With the place like this. Like a man decorated it."

Ephaltus looked around. "It's always looked like this, even when I was an apprentice."

"Exactly!"

"Well, you don't live in it as much as you sleep in it. When you are Tourney Master, you will spend ninety-five years asleep. I don't see the point."

"And those ninety-five years will be in a comfortable place I decorated. Even if the time I am awake is the only time I am conscious of it. I want those waking years to be comfortable."

"All right, it's your Earth Chamber after this tournament." He decided to use this opportunity to talk to her about his journey. "Marlee, are you comfortable enough to hold things down here and with the mages while I run an errand?"

Marlee instantly brimmed with excitement and then acted subdued, "You would trust me with everything?"

"If you can remember to recalibrate the Ocularius Magnus, then yes."

"Oh, I can! What kind of errand and how long will you be gone?"

"I am afraid it's a lengthy one. I may be gone for a few weeks. There will also be travel time involved. I won't be gone long enough to be missed; I don't think. I realize I have duties here." He glanced at the dryad who was frowning. She changed her expression when he looked at her. "But I also realize that I have a competent assistant who can handle things temporarily this time around." Marlee beamed. "Besides, the dryads are here to help you too should you need them."

"I will make you proud," she said.

"Well. I should hope so, but if all goes well, you shouldn't have anything to make me proud about, as it were." He winked at Marlee. "You remember what I told you to do if you should need me?"

"Yes, I remember."

"Good. He rummaged through some of his belongings near his favorite chair. I might need my reading glasses and pipe." He tucked the two items away in the robes of his pocket.

"You are leaving now?" Marlee asked.

"No time like the present. The journey is long, and I would like to get there and back as soon as I can."

"Are any of the mages near where you're traveling? You can use one of them to travel to so your journey time is not so long."

"No, I am afraid I will have to do this one by foot. None of the mages are off to the south that I know of at this hour." He put his finger to his nose. "Wait a moment. Where is the Black Mage?"

"Last I checked, she was in Emlestra in the kingdom of Craessa."

"Yes... Yes, that will do. I can go to her. She is about halfway to my destination. I will gather my provisions and use the orb in the Arsenal. Good call apprentice."

Marlee smiled triumphantly.

∞

If he was on tournament business, Ephaltus could travel to just about anywhere in the six kingdoms, via the portal spell, but on this personal quest, he was going to have to take the long way just like anybody else. The gods did not want any unnecessary arcane magic floating around in the kingdoms. When Ephaltus arrived in Emlestra, the first thing he noticed was the Black Mage, who had changed her appearance for the better, was hand in hand with a young man. He scowled to himself and wondered why Marlee had not mentioned the man to her. Romantic interludes might be problematic and thwart the efforts of the Tourney Master with the preparations for the tournament. He would have to talk with his apprentice upon his return. He was loath to do anything about it now. He was on a mission.

His best bet to get to the Broken Lands quickly was to join a caravan heading to the river in the west. He could then take a boat down the river to the small port at the southernmost coast of Craessa. From there, the island to the ruins he sought could be reached by ship. Perhaps he could pay a captain to drop him off after the ship was underway to the Southern Kingdoms. He watched as Thessa kissed the man she was with, making him cringe. "By the gods, I need to put a stop to this." He gathered himself up and proceeded toward Thessa with his staff in hand. He did not wish to be seen, so he used his spell discreetly to un-pants the young man. When the trousers were done leaving the man standing in his undergarments, Thessa backed away from him as he scooped up his trousers from his knees and hastily tied them back on. All the while, people around them were laughing and pointing. Thessa looked his way, but Ephaltus turned to avoid her gaze as quickly as he could. She didn't seem to notice him as she followed the humiliated man into the alleyway. Ephaltus knew the incident would not keep them apart, but it might make Thessa question who she is seen with in public. Maybe she would even think he was a bit of a dolt.

After disrupting Thessa's romantic interlude, Ephaltus went to the trade office to inquire about a caravan route. After talking with the trade master, he found that the only caravan route headed south was one going to the southern port city of Crysinnia. He knew it would be slower than by boat, but the port city was closer to the ruins of Dusanti, the island where he was ultimately headed. He paid the trade master his fare plus a fair tip, and the man gave him his rite of passage papers for the caravan master. He would also have to give the caravan master some money to ensure he rode the route comfortably. Travel by caravan was expensive, but far safer than traveling alone. Southern Craessa was notorious for bandits due to the trade routes and the island hideouts of the Broken Lands.

Ephaltus handed off his one bag to the driver of an open goods wagon and climbed aboard, sitting on top of some wooden crates containing jars of pickled this or that.

"Excuse me, driver, but have you driven this route many times?"

"Oh, yes. Have been on road many times." The man said with a thick southern, broken Eastialind accent.

"How long is the route?"

"Excuse?"

"How long until we reach Crysinnia?"

"Oh, many days. We stop on the way to deliver goods. Maybe take month."

"Splendid." Ephaltus said sarcastically.

"What do you expect? This caravan is not speedy. You should take horse next time."

"Friend, where I'm going a horse would not be practical. There will be no place to stable it or take care of it."

"Then sit tight one month."

Ephaltus leaned back against another wood crate and settled in for the long ride south. "I wonder if the gods would even notice if I used the portal spell?"

"What say you?"

"Nothing, sir. Travel on."

A week into the trip Ephaltus had poured over the parchments and clues that lead to the ruins in the Broken Lands more times than he would care to count. It was on the eighth day that he pinpointed what he speculated was the right island and the right spot to look on the island. All throughout the second week, he rode along stoically as the driver and the other wagons in the caravan stopped at one village after another, dwindling the remaining crates down until at last the only crates left on his wagon were for the city of Crysinnia.

It was during the third week a man rode up from the south warning the lead caravan driver of a gang of bandits in the area robbing passers-by. They were a little over a week from Crysinnia, which would put them deep in bandit territory. The air grew noticeably heavier with humidity and there was the faint smell of the sea blowing in from the southwest, followed by the heavy dark clouds of a storm in the distance.

"We stop when finds shelter or trees to hide under." Ephaltus' driver called back to him. "Storm coming fast."

"All right, what about bandits? I have heard they like to take advantage of situations like this?"

"Can not travel in storm. Have to risk it." He replied.

Ephaltus climbed the rock wall of the ruin and found himself staring down at a steep incline to a still mostly intact stone building. The door had long ago rotted off, but a large stone blocked the entrance none the less. He slipped while trying to lower himself down the incline and slid on his backside all the way down the wall to the stone enclosure. He stood with the help of his staff and looked at the stone to see if he could circumvent it. He could not.

"Aside!" He said as he waved his staff in the air. The stone rolled aside as the top of Ephaltus' staff glowed an ominous purple color. He entered the chamber and commanded his stall to continue to glow so he would have light. At the back of the chamber was a stone door, and on the floor, there was a mosaic of tile. The pattern looked familiar to him, so he leaned down to clean the dust of one to get a batter look at it. When he did, it shattered, revealing the floor as a facade. Any pressure put onto the tiles and they would collapse into a pit filled with sharpened wooden poles. He touched his staff to the next, intact tile. "Solidify," he said. The tiles had a faint glow wash over all of them up to the door. He could now walk across them with ease. "No one has ever been in this fool place." He murmured. "Why the traps? I think it's a bit obsessive for a shrine."

"Grumpiness will get you nowhere." A disembodied voice sounded out. Ephaltus thought he heard it coming from behind the stone door.

"All right, who in the two hells are you, then?" he asked acidly.

"Hmm, temper, temper."

"Well, I'm waiting."

"I am the guardian of the knowledge."

"Of course you are. It's always something. Who put you here, why did they put you here, and what knowledge do you guard?"

"The who is not important, the why I thought you would guess, and the what you already know."

Ephaltus pointed his staff at the door, "If you are close to the door, I suggest you back away."

The door opened before Ephaltus could cast his spell.

"No need to destroy my door. You may enter."

Ephaltus pointed his staff at the floor. "Reveal," he said. Nothing happened.

"You are safe," the voice said.

Cautiously, Ephaltus entered the chamber. At the opposite end of the room was a shelf of books, scrolls, and parchment. Before the shelf, to the right of it, was a large raven perched on a stone ledge. "You're a bird?"

"A Raven." He answered. "They wanted an owl competitor of mine, but I killed him before they could reach out and recruit him, so I got the job."

"Brutal." Ephaltus said.

"He was not a very sharp fellow. Don't pity him."

"Let me state my business here and I will be off, or do you already know why I am here?"

"What, you think I read minds? I have no idea why you're here. I assume you found something that led you here to seek the knowledge I keep."

"Do you have knowledge of the seventh god?"

"Whoa, that kind of knowledge will cost you dearly."

"All right, what's the cost?"

The raven cocked its head, "I don't know. I do not have that knowledge here."

Ephaltus took a step closer to the bird, "Then why am I talking to you? I should roast you where you perch and eat your carcass for supper. I'm in no mood for your games."

"But, if you would listen to me without making silly threats, I know where the knowledge is you seek."

"Yes, where? Another trick or clever reply?"

The raven glided off its perch and flew to the floor. On the floor it grew into a young woman in black robes with a hood over her, from what Ephaltus could see, a head of brown hair.

"Go home Tourney Master and prepare for the tournament." The one called Raven turned her back on the Tourney Master.

"I will not! I have traveled too far and risked too much."

She stopped and swiveled, "You have not risked enough."

"Then let me risk some more." He pointed his staff at the woman and let loose his arcane lightning. The one called raven waved off his spell. She cupped her hands and thrust them forward in a pushing motion. Ephaltus flew back into the wall next to the stone door.

"Your spells are weak, old man. I am a guardian of the gods."

Ephaltus stood, "I am also a guardian of the gods. I am the Tourney Master." He redoubled his efforts, and the Raven was taken off guard as the lightning from his staff struck her down. She stood without so much as a scratch and approached him. He instinctively backed away as she came closer.

She stood inches from his face, "I told you the knowledge you seek is not here. I do not guard it."

"Then what is all this *risk* business you speak of then?"

"Truth."

"Truth?"

"Yes, truth. You will have to make a sacrifice for that kind of knowledge. I can tell you were to go to look for what you seek, but that is all."

"Wait, then what knowledge do you guard?"

"Now you are asking of me questions I may answer."

"Well?"

She eyed him for a long moment, "Come back here to me should you find what you seek, the seventh god. My knowledge will be of use to you only then."

"All right, where do I look now?"

"The knowledge you seek is east, beyond the six kingdoms in the Sunken Lands. You must go there and submit to the guardian and make your sacrifice, your payment."

"What do I sacrifice?"

"Ask the guardian there, it will tell you. I am not privy to such things. I have my own depository of knowledge here to keep."

"A trick, again?"

The raven moved away from him, "Ah, there is your risk. You must decide for yourself if what I tell you is a trick or the truth."

"Why are you guardians always speaking in riddles? I am also a guardian, and I don't mince words. I tell it straight."

The raven chuckled, "I wonder if you actually believe that? Should I talk to your apprentice? I'd wager she would have a different opinion."

"I will ignore the fact you just referred to her as she, which indicates you know more of my business than you should. I never said my apprentice was female. Nevertheless, I will travel to the Sunken Lands, but be warned if this is a trick I will return, and you will not think my spells are so weak then."

"Such threats do not concern me. Be gone from my presence."

Ephaltus closed his eyes as he felt his body move as if pushed by a strong wind, and then he found himself standing on the beach of the island north of the ruins.

Chapter 16
Cracks in the Marble

Tanyth Veridian and Sir Danton rode their death steeds into a heavily wooded area where the light crept through the upper branches but dissipated to near nothing by the time they reached the thick brush at the base of the trees. The path they rode was passable. Soon the underbrush gave way to a vine covered metal gate half off its hinges. The gate was once an opulent spectacle with lavish designs and the name Sperion in large metal letters arranged in a circular pattern at its crest. Beyond the gate the path curved into an overgrown garden and finally into a marble walkway which had long ago cracked with age. The dark castle at the end of the walk was covered in vines and surrounded by unkept bushes and shrubs. The entranceway was beyond two enormous metal doors. Tanyth led Danton through the doors where freshly lit torches lined a lavish foyer. He glanced behind them as the door began to close to see about ten or more of the blood feeders they had created stumbling up the walk.

"What is this place?" Danton asked in his unusual scratchy voice.

"The Sperion family were cousins to the Veridians, my family. This is a house used before my race was known as dark elves and went underground for the most part. Now, worshipers of Cassany come here and Cassany herself resides in these hallowed halls for much of the year. She is here now." He pointed to a statue of a winged man with a spear, "There she is as a man, the winged god. She often changes her appearance and is currently a woman figure. The Black Mage's power of deception stems from the winged goddesses' ability to alter her appearance and even her gender."

They entered into a larger chamber that had once been a solarium and passed beyond it into a ballroom where Cassany had another throne set up. She was sitting watching them as they entered.

"My goddess." Tanyth said bowing, "I hope you have not been waiting too long."

"I have just now arrived." Cassany said in her booming feminine voice. "Ah, Sir Danton. You have been a busy bee of late. If my Black Mage will not create the evil, I need to roam this land, I can certainly count on my one and only Sanquinator."

Sir Danton bowed, "It has been... fun, my goddess."

"My goddess? So, you have decided to forsake your goddess, Benera, for me?"

"Benera is your ally. She will understand. Your ways always were more in line with mine. I like the power you have given me. Benera would never have granted me this power."

"No, she would not have. She might even be a little cross with me for steeling you away from your Blue Mage father."

"The fact is, I have not cared for her for years. I was lost until you found me, goddess."

"You flatter."

"It's the truth."

"Why couldn't you be my Black Mage? This could have been so much easier. Had she not created you through me, I would have you kill her and take her place. But, alas, I am stuck with her for the time being. All I can hope is our plan is successful and we convert her in time to adequately train her."

Tanyth rose from his bow, "Where is she? Is she still in Emlestra?"

"She is." Cassany said. "Once she finds out I have tricked her in order to make you, she will surely seek you out. It is time for you two to go to Emlestra and confront her."

"Forgive me, my goddess, but why would we risk going to her when by your own estimation she is seeking to Destroy Sir Danton? Wouldn't that be unwise?" Tanyth asked.

"She will not kill him. I have guarded against such things in all my Black Mages. She will revere him. In fact, the sight and presence of him will ignite the fire inside her to begin her sacrifices to me. It will entice her to create more of the evil creatures and pit them against my brother and sister gods' creations. She is close to the edge now; Sir Danton will send her over. I need him to go there."

"I see." Tanyth said.

"Have you procured the poison I asked for, Veridian?"

"The Green Mage would not make it for me."

"You must talk her into it. You can't just ask her. You have to find a way to make her do it for you. I want dominance over her. She is the enemy and I need her to submit. Get her to make the poison." Cassany's face contorted into an evil grin, "I hear her sister is the apprentice to Ephaltus. I have seen her through the great lens. She is alone quite a lot these days, and she has a habit of not calibrating the machine. Ephaltus is home at the moment, but the last time he left for some time. Wait until he leaves again and go after her. That will convince the Green Mage to do what you say."

"A brilliant plan, my goddess." Tanyth bowed again.

"When you go to Emlestra, release your blood feeders, and let them roam freely over the lands. Take none of them with you. Too many in Emlestra will bring unwanted attention. I just want you and Danton there."

"We will travel at once." Tanyth said.

"Wait, there is one more point of order." Cassany raised her hand and Sarren, as a cat, appeared. Cassany returned her to her human form. "Bend the knee, Sarren." Sarren went to her knees. "Report to me."

Sarren coughed and cleared her throat, "Thessa just left the room!"

"So, she didn't see my portal. Report!"

"Thessa's mother, the Red Mage, is in Emlestra, and so is the Grey Mage. I thought perhaps they were just traveling though, but they have been in the city for a while now."

"And Thessa?"

"She has not revealed herself to them. She believes it will cause her mother pain."

"Hmm, Hana must have heard of a girl of Thessa's former appearance in the city and is searching for her, not realizing she no longer has that visage."

"There's more. Thessa has met someone. A young man who seems to have taken quite a liking to her."

"There you go, Tanyth. I told you she would get more attention. There is yet another path you may take."

"Yes, my goddess. I may be able to use that information to our advantage. When do you want us to leave for Emlestra?"

"I want you to end up there, but I don't want you to go there just yet. There is still work to be done." She turned to Sarren, "I want you to keep Thessa in Emlestra at all costs. We need more time to prepare."

"But, she is preparing to leave. She believes that the vampires Danton is creating need to be destroyed." Sarren said.

Cassany wrinkled her upturned nose, "Then it is your job to stop her. Keep her there."

"Yes, Goddess." Sarren said. Cassany returned her to a cat and dismissed her back through a portal. "Now, the two of you must continue with your work. I want an army of blood feeders and I want you to control and lead them."

"Forgive me, goddess, but won't the other gods get nervous with us building such an army?" Tanyth asked.

"More than likely, yes. By the time they realize what's happening, it will be far too late. I will handle the meddling of my brothers and sisters. You just keep building the army without rousing too much suspicion. We don't want to alert anyone. Keep to the shadows and outer villages where news travels slowly. Remember, stay away from the bigger towns and cities." Sir Danton stared off into the distance and did not seem to be paying much attention. "Come here, Danton." Cassany commanded. He complied. "Since the Black Mage made you, I can now do this." She touched his forehead, and a sharp band of dark energy invaded his head. "There, the very next one you turn will be a Sanquinator like you. Choose wisely." She addressed Tanyth, "With two of them, you should be able to build faster."

"Thank you, goddess."

"Now, find another Sanquinator, then continue your task. In a few days travel to Emlestra and carry out the plan. Don't dawdle or wait too many days to go to Emlestra. I do not have faith in Sarren. She will not be able to keep Thessa there for long, and the opportunity to have the Red, Grey, and Black mages in one place is amazing. If you do well, you will uncover their plans too. Now go, do my bidding."

The two bowed and thanked her before turning and leaving the overgrown castle.

Chapter 17
Danse Macabre

Thessa woke up the day after she had decided to get rid of the blood feeders and reluctantly leave Gaelyn behind. Ready for action, she was determined to stop Danton from creating anymore blood feeders somehow. Cassany may have tricked her, but she was going to end it no matter how hard Sarren said the job would be. Thessa remembered what it was like to be a vampire, hiding in the shadows and forced to kill out of necessity. She would simply keep her experience in mind when she had to destroy them, not let them go. She would not look at it as a negative. She would think of it as a merciful endeavor.

She was deep in her thoughts of finding the blood feeders that she jumped at the sound of a knock on her door. Even Sarren jumped off the window seal and headed beneath the bed. The knock came again, and Thessa stood there in a moment of hesitation.

"Thessa, are you in there?" Came a loud whisper through the door. "It's me, Gaelyn. I don't mean to intrude. I will go if you are uncomfortable with me being here."

Thessa opened the door, "I am not uncomfortable. This is just unexpected. What are you doing here?"

"I thought you should know that I will be leaving this afternoon and in case I didn't see you, I didn't want you to think I just up and disappeared without saying goodbye."

"Come on in." She opened the door wider. He entered. "Where are you going?"

He sat in a chair Thessa indicated, "Some of the dock workers were chosen to travel by ship to Riverview to the south to help with the unloading of a river barge."

"I am sorry to see you go. I appreciate you stopping by to tell me. I would have been wondering where you had gotten off to if you had of just left."

"I know you would." He paused, "I really like you, Thessa, and I would like to see more of you if that is at all possible. I should be back the day after tomorrow sometime in the evening. Perhaps we could have a meal together again the day after I return?"

Thessa met eyes with Sarren, who was still under the bed and softened. She wanted to tell him she could not see him anymore, that she was also planning to leave Emlestra, but Sarren's gaze made her rethink her decision.

There is a way for you to check on the blood feeders from here. What would it hurt to stay around here for a few more days? You have never had someone to care for you like this man obviously does.

"I would like that, Gaelyn. I had planned to leave soon as well, but I suppose I could stay around for a few more days."

Gaelyn stood and took her hands in his, "That's wonderful. I was so afraid you would not be here when I returned."

"Why would you be afraid of that?" She asked.

"Because you are staying in an inn and you are not from around here. I thought if I disappeared you might think I had not cared for you and left as well."

"I will stay until you return. I promise."

"That's good news." He went for the door, "Do you promise?"

She giggled awkwardly, "I do."

He grinned and left the room. She heard a cheerful bit of whistling as he made his way down the corridor to the stairs.

You have made him very happy.

Thessa was worried, "Yes, but why wasn't I strong enough to tell him I am leaving?" Her brow wrinkled and she rubbed her forehead with the palm of her hand, "By the way, why are you trying so hard to convince me to stay here when last night you were ready to help me find the blood feeders?"

When I saw how much he liked you, I remembered you can keep tabs on the blood feeders with your mage powers. I will show you. Also, even if Sir Danton creates ten more of the creatures while you wait here, they will be just as easy to kill as the first ten.

Thessa nodded, "Yes, you're right. The odds of all the fiends being together all at once are slim. I can still round them up, regardless." She became thoughtful and changed her tone, "Just out of curiosity, how do I sense them?"

We wait until dark so we have the shadows to hide us, and I will teach you.

"Do you think there might be one in Emlestra?"

Possibly, we will find out tonight. If there is one out there, it will not be active until dark, anyway.

The rest of the day moved along without incident. Both Thessa and Sarren had a nice meal of fish for lunch and beef for supper. Thessa took advantage of the inn's steam room and bathhouse. She had never seen a steamroll before. It was a large wooden structure next to the baths with a bunch of fire heated stones in the center occasionally doused with water to create steam. She didn't really have a use for it but she tried it, anyway. The Bath was soothing.

When night fall finally came, Thessa and Sarren ventured out into the streets of Emlestra.

The way you sense the abominations is to clear your mind and search with your feelings for something living but not alive.

"What? That makes no sense."

You know it does. You were one and your mother brought you back to the living.

"Right, I remember the feeling. She searched out into the city. She had a difficult time at first, but then suddenly she zeroed in on something, "There *is* one in the city!"

Good, now use your magic to see the trail of the thing. You should concentrate on it and the path will be revealed.

She concentrated and then opened her eyes. A trail of faint light floated just above the ground. "I see it!"

Follow it!

Thessa followed the trail until she came up on a young man keeping to the shadows. She followed the trail of the vampire with her abilities into a darkened street, through an alleyway and into the Main Street of Emlestra. The streets were mostly deserted at this time of night. She wondered if Gaelyn's ship had come in safely and she thought she might go down the docks later and check to see if it's moored there after she dispatched this blood feeder, of course. Realizing she was distracted, she concentrated on the fiend again and finally saw it again as it was lurking in the shadows near another one of the alleyways. She moved stealthily toward the alley when she spotted movement ahead in the street. Several men in sailor's clothing carrying long sacks over their shoulders were disbursing in different directions. They had come from the docks. Thessa froze as the fiend was eyeing them from his place in the dark. She had to warn them. She took one step into the light and to her horror saw Gaelyn trudging up the street. She tried to move back into the shadows before he saw her, but it was too late. He called out to her.

"Thessa? Is that you?"

Thessa stepped out of the darkness, all the while keeping a wary eye on the blood feeder perched in the alleyway. "It's me."

"You came to see me home?"

He seemed so genuinely happy to see her she couldn't say no. "Yes, but I wasn't sure which way you would be coming into town, or where for that matter. Why don't you stay there, and I will come to you? Don't you move." She kept her tone calm and steady. His happy demeanor cut Thessa to the core. He began to move toward her again.

"No, stay there, Gaelyn. I will come to you!" He either didn't hear her or he didn't listen. Thessa watched as Gaelyn made his way to her, oblivious to the danger. The torch-lit streets were too dark and afforded many shadows all around. His smile struck her in the heart as she saw Danton in the darkness. He was maneuvering behind him, stalking him.

"Gaelyn, look out!" She called, and he stopped and faced Danton as he came from the shadows at a full, supernatural speed. Without so much as a thought, she lashed out with a purple tinged black ribbon of magic, the most powerful she could muster, at Danton. It struck him and knocked him far, fast, and hard against the nearby building. "Gaelyn, run to me!"

Gaelyn complied and took off in a sprint toward her, which is when ten other blood feeders came from out of the shadows. Lights began to appear in windows as the inhabitants of the houses and businesses lining the street were roused from sleep by the noise. Tanyth rose from the spot where he landed and moved again toward Gaelyn. Thessa tried to stop him, but Tanyth stayed behind Gaelyn, putting the man between himself and Thessa so she could not blast him back again.

"Move Gaelyn, get out of the way!" Gaelyn looked behind him and Thessa moved forward, knowing that when he saw Tanyth, Gaelyn would slow down enough for Tanyth to catch him.

Danton stepped out of the shadows and knocked Thessa to the ground as Tanyth caught up with Gaelyn and put his dagger to the man's throat. "Resurrect this!" He cut Gaelyn's throat and let him fall to the ground.

"No!" Thessa pleaded, but it was too late. She reached him and held the blood gushing from his neck. He was not dead yet. She used what power she had and willed the wound to close, but it did not. A moment later she caught the familiar scent of her mother close by her. She looked up to see Hana beside her. Hana was controlling Gaelyn's blood and making it flow back into him. Once the blood had returned, she pulled out a green vial and added a drop to the wound on Gaelyn's neck. It closed up, and he gasped for breath.

Briefly, Thessa looked up to see Asleth using a force shield to send the blood feeders away, including Tanyth. Gaelyn shook his head, probably to clear it to what just happened, twisted his face into expressions of complete horror while looking at Thessa and Hana, and he began to quickly back away.

"Wait, Gaelyn, let me explain." Thessa called after him.

He ran toward the alley where Danton abruptly leaped out of the shadows and sunk his teeth into his neck. Thessa could not believe her eyes. Tanyth smiled with satisfaction and took a final blow from Asleth before scurrying away into the darkness of another alleyway. Danton dragged Gaelyn into the darkness as Thessa ran toward them. When she reached the alley within seconds they had already gone, completely disappeared somewhere into the dark. She ran down the alley until it ended and turned onto the parallel street, but there was no sign of either Gaelyn nor Danton.

She gazed at the shadow where Sarren had been hiding, "What do I do, Sarren?" There was no answer. "Sarren? Where has she gone?"

Chapter 18
Memorial

Sarren was watching Thessa run into the alley, after Sir Danton and Gaelyn, when she felt the now familiar pull of Cassany's portal. She blinked and then she was in the twisted throne room in the estate in the woods. Cassany was nearly giddy with excitement. *You nearly got me caught again. I was with Thessa in the street.* Sarren lamented.

"Forget about that. You were not seen." Cassany waved her hand and Sarren returned to her human form. "I need your report. I hope you have some good news for me."

Sarren lowered her head, "They were successful if you intended for Thessa's gentleman friend to become a blood feeder."

Cassany clapped her hands, "Excellent! That should get her mad enough to seek revenge. She is one step closer to being the Black Mage I am hoping for to win this tournament."

"If I May, it was a mistake. She didn't know him all that well. She liked him very much, but waiting until she loved him might have been a better choice."

Cassany's joyful grin soured into a deep frown, "It would not have mattered much. She merely needed a push, not a hard shove. Now, Sir Danton and Tanyth can take their men to the arena and focus on the next part of my plan. Thessa will mope and mourn her loss with her mother and then at some point ask you how to make her own blood feeders. What I need you to do is tell her that Danton and Tanyth are headed toward the arena to attack Marlee so they can force the Green Mage to make the poison I need."

"You want me to tell her?"

"Yes, like you are a good little servant. Make sure she trusts you first and then tell her you have been forced to meet with me and I told you the entire plan. She will try to warn the Green Mage but tell her it's too late for that. Tell her I told you the Green Mage already knew about the attack and is heading to the arena, which she is. I sent word to her that Thessa was planning something to harm Marlee. It is time to get Thessa on her way to using her powers and end this ridiculous alliance with Teoni, The Green Mage." She leaned in toward Sarren, "I know you have a black heart, Sarren, I know you are not getting attached to the person who robbed you of the Black Mage you once were, but do not even think about betraying me or I will make you regret it in ways you can't possibly understand but may be able to imagine. Do as I say, and I will reward you by setting you free as a human, no more Thessa and no more cat."

"I understand goddess."

"Good." She waved her hand and returned Sarren into a cat. "Go back now and tell Thessa, but not too soon. Wait until she is vulnerable enough to believe you. If all goes to plan, I get what I want, you will get what you want, and I will be one step closer to winning the tournament this time. Now, go." She waved her hand again and Sarren went through the portal back to Thessa.

∽

Thessa was sitting at entrance to the alleyway with her head in her hands. Sarren looked around but did not see Hana or Asleth. *Where did your mother and Asleth go?*

"There you are. Where did you go?"

Cassany used a portal to bring me before her. She has been using me to spy on you.

"What?"

I meant to tell you earlier, but I was afraid she would be watching me somehow. I am not afraid now after what she told me. You need to know her twisted plan.

"Right now, I don't care. She can do whatever she thinks she needs to do."

You should care. It involves Gaelyn, Tanyth, and Danton. She is sending them to attack the arena and Marlee to force the Green Mage to make her some poison. The Green Mage has refused, so Cassany is sending them to use Marlee as leverage to Get what she wants.

"Why does a god need poison?"

First off, she is a Demigod and not a full-fledged god. Second, she is planning to use it on a fellow demigod. It won't kill, but it will put the demigod out long enough to make a single move against his or her mage without them knowing. You didn't answer my question.

"Some of the people came out and saw Asleth fighting in the streets. So, he and Hana, mother, went to the Reeve's office to clear things up. Hana told me to stay here and wait for her return." She rubbed the cold from her hands, "I need to warn Teoni then."

She already knows and is on her way to stop Tanyth from getting to the arena.

"And you learned all this from Cassany?"

Yes! Suddenly, Sarren worried she had spilled the news too soon. Maybe she had not begun to trust her as much as she thought.

"Why would she tell *you* her plans? Is she counting on you telling me? Is that it?"

She didn't I overheard her telling them to someone else involved. she lied.

"Yes, who?"

I have no idea. I never got to see their face. They were wearing a hooded cloak.

Thessa wiped her eyes, and that's when Sarren realized she had been crying. "If she wants to push me into making blood feeders and is using you to do it, then she is about to be very happy. I am going to do it my way, though."

Sarren thought to herself, *Does she know Cassany put me up to this? How would she?*

"I doubt Cassany told you all these secrets knowing you might run to me and blab in good faith. Either she is using you or you are in on her plan. I still don't completely trust you. I mean, I did technically kill you and take the Black Mage from you. Why would you be loyal to me, right! Still, I know somewhere in your twisted thoughts you might have the capacity to care. Still, I believe Cassany is using you to bait me into making an army to go after Tanyth."

I have gotten over all that nonsense. I am loyal to you.

"Still, whether what you say is you trying to be loyal to me or if you are still being loyal to Cassany, she is about to get her wish. I want you to tell me how to make vampires, blood feeders."

I will teach you to the best of my ability.

"I know you will. It's in your best interest." She took a long breath, "Actually, I have to admit it's in the best interest for all three of us." She picked herself up. "I'm sure you want to be human again, I want the power to stop Tanyth and Danton, and Cassany wants a trained Black Mage."

Sarren felt a sudden kinship with Thessa at that moment. She was wiser and more intelligent than she had given her credit to be. *Then I think I should point out to you something I observed. Something you are not thinking about in order to prove my sincerity.*

"What am I not thinking about?"

Your mother could have saved Gaelyn. She still can. She can bring life back into him as she once did for you.

"I thought that was a one-off occurrence."

Oh, no, her power is blood and blood is life. She can change the taint back and purge it from the body.

"She didn't have time."

Asleth can manipulate gravity and force. He could have made Danton too heavy to walk or contained him in a force shield. They let them go, and they let Gaelyn go with them.

"Why? What would they do that?"

Look what happened. They must have figured out who you were based on your ribbon spell and the blood feeders. They must know you are Thessa.

"No, I can't accept that. How would they know?"

I am sorry, Thessa, but you know deep down it's true. Sarren could see in Thessa's eyes that she was getting to her. While it was true that Hana saved Thessa, she had no idea if she could have done it for anyone else who was not her direct kin. The important part is she convince Thessa to believe it.

"Your words are venomous!" Thessa spat. Sarren held her breath. "But there is some truth to what you say. Perhaps my mother does know, and perhaps she could have saved him. Maybe she still can. She will return shortly, and I will ask her."

Chapter 19
A Grave Mistake

Thessa watched Sarren's movements as she spoke. She just could not trust the former Black Mage with information. She trusted her to teach her, but she knew it was in her best interest to do so. Other than that, she did not trust her to be truthful, especially when it came to information from Cassany. She had not doubted she was talking to Cassany and reporting, but why would she betray the goddess and tell her anything. It had to be a deception. But even if it were a deception, Thessa vowed no matter how long it took or no matter how many times someone tells her it is the wrong way to think, she would hunt down Tanyth Veridian and destroy him.

On a whim, she tried to sense the surrounding fiends again. She thought perhaps she could sense Danton or even Gaelyn. If she could find them, maybe she could have her mother bring Gaelyn back. She reached out with her dark powers, but she felt nothing... at first. After a few moments, she did feel one of the blood feeders still lurking around. She had no way to know who the field was, but she somehow felt it was not the two she hoped it would be. She willed it gone. There came a sharp cracking noise, and she sucked in a breath like all the air had suddenly been knocked out of her. When she caught her breath, she felt the thing die and then came the surge of power. It was gradual at first, but then it intensified over time until it abruptly burst within her. That's when she knew that the more death magic she absorbed, the more powerful she would become. She suspected instinctively that it worked this way, but now she was certain. A few moments after she felt the power grow within her, Hana returned.

"I wanted to come back and check on you, Zarina." Hana said.

Thessa was not in the mood to keep up with appearances, "I think you know that's not my name. How long have you known? I mean, you say you were looking for your daughter, but you keep lingering here in Emlestra."

"I wasn't sure until I saw you use your death magic. The spell looked like one I saw Sarren cast. Plus, Sarren had been a man the whole time I knew her until I found out she was really a woman who had the ability to change her appearance. It was not a difficult leap from there." Hana reached out and took a strand of Thessa's white highlighted hair. "I like the look you chose."

Thessa fought back the tears she felt welling up inside her, "Why did you leave me?"

"I didn't. That was the Tourney Master's doing. I tried to go right back, but you had gone." She cleared her throat, but Thessa knew she too was holding back tears. "Say, I want to ask you something. When we returned to the cavern, Tovo was there dead, but Sarren was gone. What happened to her?"

Thessa stopped her and pointed to the cat wandering around the street sniffing and exploring, "*That* is Sarren."

Hana giggled, "What? You didn't?"

Thessa shrugged, "I needed a teacher, so I had Cassany make her into a cat. I always wanted a cat. She can talk to me in my mind."

"That is brilliant and the perfect punishment for that pompous ass. I am glad you found a way to keep her close to teach you but far enough away not to harm you."

"Oh, she's still dangerous. She could hurt me if she wanted to, but if she ever wants to be a human again, she has no choice but to do as I say. I can never fully trust her of course."

"Well, I still think it's wonderful. I don't think I could have done it. I think I would have left her dead."

"Mother, I want to ask you something important. Could you have saved, or can you save Gaelyn, the man taken by Sir Danton?"

"I don't understand. Who is Sir Danton?"

"He was the vampire who dragged off the man, Gaelyn, in the alley."

"Gaelyn is now a blood feeder?"

"I assume so. Can you bring him back like you did me?

"I don't know. I've never tried it on anyone but you. I'm sorry, it never crossed my mind while it was happening."

"Would you try it if you get the chance, for me?"

"Of course I will, Thessa." She smiled lovingly, "Now tell me how you're doing. What's it like to be the Black Mage and what we should we do next? How do we get you out of this?"

Thessa watched Sarren wander back up and sit a few feet away. She calmly began licking her fur like any other normal cat.

"Mother, I think I sealed my fate when I took the Black Mage away from Sarren. I don't want to turn back. I think I will embrace being the Black Mage and use this death magic to my advantage. Everyone close to me is trying to deceive me. I finally found someone who cared for me, even if might have been just because of the way I look now, and he was taken from me."

"Revenge? Is that wise?" Hana asked.

"I don't know." She peered at the cat who was obviously listening in on their conversation. "You tell me, Sarren!" She looked intently at the cat as she continued to lick her fur.

Tell you what? Revenge? Sure, go for it! I would.

"This is Hana, Sarren. *The* Hana.

Sarren stopped licking her fur long enough to examine the Red Mage then she returned to her task.

Yes, so?

Thessa stood, her eyes boiling red. A red mist began to form around her, writhing in red ribbons that alternated with black.

"What are you doing, dear?" Hana asked. She appeared unnecessarily alarmed.

Thessa lashed out with her magic, knocking Hana on her backside. She sucked in the power around her and lashed out again. "I don't think this is very funny." Thessa shouted. Sarren was up with her back arched and the hair standing up on her back. Thessa took a step and punted her across the road. "I have been so stupid! Hana would have tried everything to save Gaelyn. She could have taken him from Danton easily."

Sarren hissed and ran back to where Thessa held Hana pinned to the ground with the red mist. *What are you talking about?*

"Sarren hates Hana. You have made a grave mistake. If this were really Hana, you would have shown your contempt for her. You acted like it was nothing to be around her. Where is Asleth? He almost never lets Hana out of his sight. I am tired of being manipulated." She began to command the red mist to crush the imposter. The woman who was Hana began to gasp, and then Thessa saw the delicate movements of the woman's hands right before she felt the white ribbons wrapping around her feet. By the time she looked down, the ribbons had yanked her feet out from under her and she fell hard to the ground. Fia stood, put her hands on her knee and gasped for breath. Hana was shocked. "Fia, you?"

"Don't blame me. It was for your own good. We need you to be the Black Mage."

"This is low, even for you. How could you?"

Cassany put her up to it. I would not blame her if I were you.

"Shut up, Sarren, I don't trust a thing you say."

"Embrace your destiny." Fia said.

"I already have!" Thessa practically shouted. "I didn't need your deceptions! I was telling the truth, I have decided to build my blood feeder army. But I will do it my way. I will not be manipulated. She reached for Fia's throat, and the White Mage backed away, "You have risked everything. If you want me to trust you in an alliance, you will never do anything like this to me ever again! The Green Mage has been kinder to me than you two have, and I am supposed to be her enemy." Thessa glanced down the street and realized the sun was about to come up and the city folk of Emlestra would be filling the streets soon. She pointed at Sarren, "You will teach me how to make blood feeders from criminals. I will find the worst people alive. The scoundrels, deceivers, thieves, rapists, and murderers. I will choose the people who deserve the curse of being a lowly blood feeder from the horrible deeds they have committed. I won't even elevate them to the status of vampire. They will be the bottom feeders of my army. You will help me find them, Sarren." She turned to Fia, "And you will go off somewhere and train with your own god and prepare to fight in the arena, because if the others are defeated and it's just you and I left you are going to need every song and every dance you can remember. I will not hold back!"

"That's the spirit!" Fia said. "Well, I think my work is done here. Farewell to you Sarren, I am happy I could help."

Thessa became incensed.

"Whoa, you better calm down, Blacky, you might pop a blood vessel or something." Fia quipped. She hurriedly and gracefully moved along down the street away from them, as if she were almost running away. She might have used the tune she was whistling for protection because Thessa wanted to lash out.

Stop, don't. Don't do anything rash. That's just her way. She is worried about you and scared of you now.

"What? No, she's not."

Yes, she is, you fool. Don't you get it?

"I guess I don't. I can't actually hurt her can I?"

You were doing so well with your insight and observations. Mages are not supposed to be able to kill each other before the tournament. Your red mist held her down, and you were crushing the life out of her. Your magic was not supposed to be able to do that. She felt real fear.

"I was angry. She pretended to be my mother all this time to deceive me into becoming who I was already becoming. Whose bright idea was that? Cassany?"

It worked. You got so angry you focused your magic in ways unheard of before. You are not supposed to be able to harm another mage like that, yet you did.

"Just because I can't kill her doesn't mean I can't beat the fire out of her does it?"

Good point. I did try to hurt your mother but not severely beat her or anything. I suppose it's something to try if the need arises.

"Don't ever do anything like that to me again, Sarren, or I will tell Cassany I no longer need you and then who knows what your fate will be then." Sarren nodded her furry little head. "We need to go back to the inn and get some sleep." We have a busy time ahead. Oh, and I do plan to find my mother, my real mother, to cure Gaelyn. I know she will try to cure him if I ask her to, even if she can't do it, she will try. The people of Emlestra began to exit their houses and go about their daily tasks as Thessa and Sarren returned to the Suckling Pig Inn.

Chapter 20
Black Mage

Thessa felt the hunger within her magnify, but she would show Cassany that she would do things her way and not follow the directives of the goddess. She would create blood feeders on her own, but they would be people who deserved the punishment. Being a blood feeder in her mind was a curse and she would only curse those she deemed appropriate; but how would she find these people? She hesitated, but finally relented that this problem was something she could share with Sarren. The former Black Mage would know where to find the worst of the worst people. Cities like Emlestra and Riverview must have unsavory areas where these people would congregate. If Cassany wanted a Black Mage, she was about to get one!

"Sarren, I want you to lead me into the worst areas of Emlestra where the criminals and murderers hang around. Can you do that?"

Yes, but why?

"I'll tell you why. If I am to be the Black Mage and release such abominations into the world, I want to curse those who really deserve it."

No, I already know your reasoning. You want bad people to suffer and not good people? But you do realize that if you make murderers and criminals into blood fiends and blood feeders, they will still retain their natures. You will create an army of undead who are difficult to control. The murders in particular may even enjoy being able to kill so efficiently.

"I will not condemn innocent people to that kind of life. I know firsthand what that life is like."

Yes, I know. Hardly a day goes by without you reminding me.

"Sarcasm? Really? Do you know where to go in this stinking city or not?"

I know where to go.

"Take me there."

It would be better to go under the cover of night where you can use the shadows. These people are not too apt to roam around in the daylight anyway. No one likes to commit crimes out in the open with plenty of light to shine on their wrongdoings.

"All right, we can wait until dark. How do I tell who the bad guys are?"

You will know. Bad guys are not like good guys, they cannot act civil forever. They may start out charming and seem like they are upstanding, but they are never able to hold on to that illusion for long. They will eventually begin to show their true nature. In fact, you can speed up the process by not falling for their charms and countering their machinations. The more they try to blend in, the more you expose them, and they will crack like eggs.

"Do you know all the places these people frequent in all the big cities?"

Naturally, some of the best blood feeders come from such places. I just never used them much because, as I said, they can be difficult to control. Once you give a murderer the tools to get away with murdering people, they tend to stop listening to you and start murdering indiscriminately. Again, even though they can be a powerful blood feeder, they can also be difficult.

"What do you do if that happens?"

It is a chore to rein them in, but it can be done. She swished her tail. *You won't like what I am about to say.*

"Get on with it."

They will kill and kill until they realize that the blood is the life, and they are overfilling themselves. They will eventually begin to realize the thrill of killing is gone and is just a means to an end. It becomes a necessity and that curbs their want and need to kill. When it becomes less fun and more of a way to live, they lose interest and began killing only for sustenance.

"So, they reach a limit? How long does that take? How many do they need to kill to realize it?"

There's the problem. Only a few reach that point because either the townsfolk have discovered them and dispatched them as vampires due to their over killing, or they kill for years before it finally seeks in if they survive long enough. I have only had two blood feeders who were murderers who survived to the point they stopped killing for fun.

"Perfect!" Thessa said. "Don't you see, that solves my problem. I can alert the townsfolk and expose them before they can do too much damage. I can use their death to further my power and then have them eliminated."

You forget they will be like your children. You will have a hard time bringing yourself to get rid of them.

"I won't be killing them. The townsfolk will."

You can't see it's the same thing? What about the people the blood feeder kills before the townsfolk takes an interest?

"If you do your job, they will probably go after other criminals."

We will go later tonight. You'll see your plan is deeply flawed.

Thessa thought about it for a moment, "No, I have decided we will leave now, but not to the bad places in Emlestra. I don't want to stay here any longer. What is the most corrupt city you have ever visited?"

That's easily King's Cross.

"Yes, but that is the capital city with the king and his guards, I would rather not go there."

There is the capital of Vestia, Talt. It's almost as corrupt as King's Cross. Then, once we visit there, we can go north to Ironhold. It's an old fort city in Adendalind rumored to be a hideout for thieves with easy access to the Vesta river.

"Could you describe it to me? I think we will travel there by spell."

Cassany will know and will probably intercept you for a meeting.

"She can do that anytime she wants. Besides, I hope she does. Maybe if she thinks I'm finally going to start obeying her murderous agenda, she will stop with the likes of Tanyth Veridian. I know what she is doing. If she thinks her plans have worked on me, maybe she will be satisfied."

Sarren stretched and yawned, *all right. I am ready when you are. I would caution you to be careful manipulating a goddess, but it would do no good, would it?*

"No."

Okay, I am ready to go. There is a clearing in the trees outside of Talt on the southern side. If you take us there, we should be safe to travel into the city relatively easily. No one would even look twice at us. I would not suggest you wear your new clothes, the ones with the straps and leafy top though. We want to blend in, not give the guards reasons to chase after you with their tongues wagging.

Thessa chuckled, "Good point. She gathered her things and used the Black Mage travel spell to get them to Talt quickly.

With a whoosh of cool air, Thessa arrived in the clearing near the city intact with her bag and Sarren close by her side. The area surrounding them was covered in thick clusters of various sized trees, bushes, and shrubs. Ahead in the distance were the spires of the city of Talt, the capital city of Vestia, and their destination. The air was colder here and far less humid. A light breeze blew in from the west.

"Where should we stay while here?"

The best inn for us would be the Hunter and Hound. I had you come to this clearing because I have a chest of coins nearby. We can visit it to pad our purse before we go into the city.

"You don't have a single coin here like you did in Emlestra?"

No, for one there is not a coin shop here and second, I would rather take coins in with us than procure them within the city walls. What happened to you in Emlestra is far more commonplace here. Keep your money hidden at all times and do not give any indication of the amount you have on you.

Thessa and Sarren walked the mile or so it took to get to the southern gate of Talt. The city was very different from Emlestra. Where the river port city of Emlestra was largely an open city without walls or too many guards, Talt was walled and at least a couple of miles away from the city docks on the Vesta River. The buildings were taller, and it had several towers and spires reaching up to the sky like great pointed fingers. The city was surrounded by woods, so the gates were wooden while the walls were a combination of wood and stone. Compared to Emlestra, the city of Talt looked cold and uninviting. She hopped inside the walls would improve her first impression of the place. There were two guards who greeted them at the gate. They were chain mail with the blue and white herald of the Taltian Eagle embroidered on the front of their tabards. They beckoned for Thessa to stop.

"What business do you have in Talt young lady? The largest of the two guards asked.

Thessa set down her bag, "I am a traveler just passing through. I thought I might patron one of your inns, the Hunter and Hound?"

"So, you are just traveling through for a day and night's stay?"

"I have never been to Talt before. I thought I might explore the shops and see what the city has to offer. I could stay a few days."

"If you plan to stay more than one day, I need to take down your name."

"My name is Zarina Deshane, and this is my cat, Sarren."

Oh, you couldn't change my name?

"Well now, I had not noticed the kitty. You might want to carry her through the streets to the inn. We have many dogs roaming around in the city and one might take the notion to make her its meal." He reached down to pat Sarren on the head.

"She will take her chances." Thessa said cheerfully. She imagined Sarren scowled at her, but the cat said nothing to her.

"Suit yourself, miss. The Hunter and Hound is down the Main Street to your left; you can't miss it."

"Thank you, kind sir," she said with a slight genuflect.

"Now, don't go gettin' into trouble or I will have to come after ya," he said.

"I won't," She replied, wondering if the guard was flirting with her. She couldn't tell. She would have to ask Sarren about it at the inn if she was paying attention. She might have been to upset at her to notice.

Sarren stayed unusually close to her legs as Thessa made her way up the street to the inn. The guard was right, it was not difficult to find. She went in, set up her payment for her accommodation, and then entered the room. It was pleasant and not at all dusty or stuffy. There was a table with two chairs, a chest of drawers with a water pitcher on top, a bed large enough for two people to sleep on comfortably, and a window with a pane big enough for Sarren to sit on and stare out. She put her things on the bed.

You could have carried me.

"Oh, don't be hurt. You killed a man; I doubt a dog will be a challenge for you."

Sarren went to the windowpane and hopped up on it. *It will be dark in a couple of hours. Are you sure you want to do this?*

"I have to stop Tanyth and appease Cassany, and I have a few reasons of my own. Yes, I want to do this. Are you going to be able to come along with me or are you scared of street dogs?"

Ha, you're funny. I will come along with you, but I expect you to take care of me should there be any trouble with canines of any type.

"It's a deal."

Chapter 21
The Way is East

When Ephaltus returned to Crysinnia, he decided the best course of action would be to secure a ride on a ship to the Sunken Lands. He had already been absent from the Arsenal of the Way for too long, and the trip back by caravan would take another month. The dryads would be furious with him if he traveled another month by ship to the Sunken Lands, and then it would probably take two months from there to return to the Arsenal. Marlee had not contacted him with any problems. Perhaps if he checked in with her, he could plan whether to travel on or return home. There was one more alternative. He could have Marlee contact the Grey Mage. Perhaps he could convince Asleth to make a portal and take him to the east coast, or even to the city of Arnost on the main island of the Sunken Lands. It would be a misuse of his power as Tourney Master, and he wasn't sure it was ethical either. Using one of the mage's powers for the personal gain of a Tourney Master was unheard of and would certainly be frowned upon at the least. He decided his desire to travel would have to wait. He needed to go back to the Arena and check in before he could finish his quest to find the seventh god and possibly discontinue the tournament all together, so he packed up his things and evoked his arcane magic to return to the Arsenal of the Way. He could return to the origin point in the arsenal as long as he was still the Tourney Master.

The end destination of the portal placed Ephaltus in the main chamber. He took his things, including the scrolls and parchments he collected in the pocket dragon chamber before he headed for his living quarters. There he found Marlee at the dining table, scribing words onto parchment paper. She was so engrossed in her work that she started when Ephaltus let the great wooden door close.

"Hey, you frightened me. How did your errand go?"

"It went well; however, I am afraid it led me to yet another long-term errand to the east. I was reluctant to travel before returning to check on things here." He glanced at her writing. "How did it go?"

"It went well. I have nothing to report. The mages are all doing fine, taking into account the tragic circumstances of some."

"It's all part of the process. I have seen Cassany do much worse to her champions in the past to get them to comply with her twisted will. The trick for us is not to interfere unless it's absolutely warranted."

"That's just it. How do we know what's warranted and what is manipulation on our part?"

"It's tough call, but essentially, if the gods or mages do something to disrupt or something that can potentially disrupt the tournament we are to step in and protect the integrity of the tournament, which is why I agreed to whisk away the Red and Grey mage after Thessa's transformation. I later realized it was a mistake, but the damage was done. We must not give into impulsive whims like that if we can help it."

Marlee nodded, "I have apologized for that."

"I realize you have. I am not chastising you again about it. You asked, and it's the only example I had floating around in my head."

"This new errand you speak of will it take you a while again?"

"I am afraid so. The quest I am on indicates the direction I must travel next is east. I thought of asking the Grey Mage for a portal to speed things up, but as an example of what we were just speaking about, it would be unethical and wrong of me to ask."

"What about the portal of the Way?"

"I could use it, but again my task is not for official business of the Tourney Master. I couldn't condone the portal's use for this."

"Isn't it? I mean tournament business? Are you not involved in a quest that may somehow affect the tournament? I don't know what you're doing other than what you said about it being for your retirement, but does it have anything to do with the tournament?"

Ephaltus rubbed the whiskers on his chin, "Hmm, I had not thought about it that way but yes, I suppose if I do find what I seek on this quest it could affect the tournament, especially the current tournament." He watched Marlee for a moment and her pleasant, understanding half grin convinced him. "It could affect you too. Where are the dryads?"

"They are around. I assume they are where they go when not here in the Earth chamber."

"Are none of them in the kitchen?"

"I'll check." She returned a few moments later. "No, it's just you and me."

"All right. I have stumbled on something. I have found evidence there may be a seventh god in exile somewhere."

Marlee's mouth gaped, "What?"

"I know. It's shocking. There may be a seventh god."

"That would be tournament business. If this god were found and decided he or she wanted a champion in the tournament, it could set off the balance of the six kingdoms, and the six mages. If you find this god, what are your intentions? Surely, you're not planning to bring this god back! Can you even do such a thing?"

"I have not decided. First, I need to find out what happened to the god."

"You haven't thought this through. As the next Tourney Master, it would be my duty to stop you as your actions could adversely affect the outcome of the tournament."

"You forget yourself, Marlee. You could only interfere if I do find and free the seventh god during the next cycle when you are actually the Tourney Master. As of this moment, I am the Tourney Master. I can do as I please. I even have the power to reinstate the seventh god in the tournament if I see fit."

"Then it would be your duty not to release the god as it may interfere with your tournament. A new god with or without a champion would make the numbers odd instead of even."

"There is a difference between finding if the god exists and freeing it. If the god is even exiled or trapped. He or she might have walked away from this world. The god may simply not wish to participate."

"Then again, they might. Where is the next clue? You said east."

"The Sunken Lands."

"So, did the Sunken Lands used to be part of the six kingdoms?"

Ephaltus stroked his chin again, "Actually yes." He became excited. He went to the bookshelf and took down a book titled the History of the Six Kingdoms. "I remember something mentioned about it in this book." He thumbed through the volume. Here it is, "The Sunken Lands used to be part of a larger kingdom called Aubria. Most of it sunk into the East Ocean. It was located in the east as part of Vestia and also as part of Craessa, the eastern area where the city of Oceanview is located, was once a part of the seventh kingdom but was annexed into Craessa after the cataclysm that caused the kingdom's destruction. Aubrians were isolationists, didn't participate in the tournament, and therefore never had a mage. The remaining surviving inhabitants of Aubria wished to be independent of the six kingdoms. Independence was granted by the King of the Six Kingdoms after the tournament that took place at the time of the old kingdom's demise. It was renamed the Sunken Lands, and the capital established as Arnost, the largest remaining city."

"If the kingdom didn't have a mage, then it might not fall under tournament business, right?"

"The book doesn't say anything about the seventh god or that the seventh god was the patron god of Aubria. The two may not be related. The seventh god may still interfere with the tournament if it is ever found or released by anyone who stumbles across the legend. Should the rumors be true, I would be wise to investigate its existence for the future integrity of the tournament."

"Do you know when you will be leaving?"

"Now that I realize I can portal to Seahorn or King's Cross on the east coast of Vestia, I imagine I will be leaving as soon as I check the Ocularius Magnus and the status of the mages and tournament."

"You will find nothing has changed. I am keeping tabs on everything and logging it all down." She indicated the parchment on which she was writing earlier. "I have been recalibrating the machine too, before you ask."

"Excellent. Keep on recording everything so I can review it later, and we will both be covered should anything detrimental arise. Also, continue with the remodeling of the arena. We want it to be in top shape for the tournament. I'm going to go see what I can see in the Ocularius Magnus. I'll return shortly." Marlee smiled and nodded.

Ephaltus calibrated the Ocularius Magnus lens and looked in on each of the mages. When he got to the Black Mage, the lens focused not on Thessa but on a shadow lurking in the dark places of the city of Emlestra. He focused in on the face when the creature showed it in the light briefly. He had seen the face before, although it was now gaunter and more sunken. He thought about it for a long moment but couldn't place it. It seems like it was connected to the Blue Mage somehow. He decided he would ask Marlee and exited the machine. The man looked like a blood feeder, and since Ephaltus was looking for the Black Mage, it made sense he would see one of her creations. When he went back to his living quarters, he found Marlee still writing.

"Has there been any developments with Thessa? I think I saw one of her blood feeders."

"She has been distraught lately."

"Her story is a tragedy, and I am afraid it will only get worse the more she fights against Cassany."

"I have not seen her creating blood feeders, though. What did you see?"

"I saw a man lurking in the shadows. When the light illuminated his face, I saw that it was sunken in and gaunt. He is unmistakably a vampire."

"What should we do about it? Will it affect the tournament?"

"It could if it comes into contact with the right people. Keep an eye on it if you can while I'm gone. We need to make sure Thessa's creations are at a minimum. Dead things tend to want to make other things dead too."

"I will."

A dryad came into the room bringing an afternoon snack of ripe fruit. Ephaltus stopped her when she passed him, "Please have the dryad smiths forge a Tourney Master ring for Marlee. Make certain they connect it with mine so she can contact me." The dryad nodded and left the room.

"You're giving me a ring?"

"It's time. You can use it to contact me through my ring and you can stop having the dryads let you into the Arsenal and Earth Chamber when I'm gone."

"Thank you!"

"I'm going to use the portal now. Be sure to watch the blood feeders and let me know immediately if anything changes."

"I will. Have a safe trip and good luck."

"Tell no one of my quest. Not even the dryads."

"All right."

"At this point it's only an investigation."

Marlee nodded again, and Ephaltus nodded back to her before he left the Earth Chamber.

Chapter 22
The Shrunken Lands

Ephaltus decided on the port city of King's Cross. He had considered Seahorn to the north since King's Cross was the capital of the six kingdoms and the home of the king himself; however, too many bored guards roamed the streets and docks of the city looking for things to do for his liking. He was in a hurry to ferry the Vestian channel to the island of the Sunken Lands, and Seahorn was much farther away. He navigated the streets successfully avoiding the guards until he at last came to the ship docks in the eastern quarter. There were guards here too, but they were too busy harassing the captains of the moored ships to notice him. How he loathed the king's guardsmen, the vicious lot of undesirables that they were. He spied a ship at the final berth with men loading crates into the hold with the designation Arn stamped on one of them. Arn stood for Arnost. He made his way to the gangplank and stepped up next to the ship. "Permission to come aboard." He said to the nearest officer.

"Who asks?" The officer replied.

"A simple traveler looking for passage to Arnost."

"You got money?"

"Of course. I would be happy to negotiate a price."

"We ain't cheap, friend. Arnost is a treacherous voyage with the cities sunken beneath the waves jutting up all over the place."

"Yes, but are you not already going there regardless of passengers?"

"You tryin' to get smart, friend?"

"No, merely pointing out the obvious."

"The odd what?"

"No, the obvious. You know what, never mind. I can pay you twenty gold."

"Twenty gold! Say, how much you carrying?"

Ephaltus learned long ago to travel with an enchanted purse. It has an infinite amount of gold, as all Tourney Masters do, but the money only appears in it to him. When anyone else looks in it, the purse appears empty. "I have about twenty gold and a bit of silver and copper. You will get the lion's share of what I brought."

"I ain't no liar!" The man was about to get physical. "I always share with the crew."

"No, it's an expression. Lion's share means you get almost all of my money."

"We are an honest crew. We will only need about fifteen of your gold. Keep your five for Arnost. You will need it there."

"All right. Fifteen it is."

"Well, come aboard then. Permission granted." He turned to a young boy swabbing the deck. "You, cabin boy."

"Yes sir?" The boy scrambled to the officer's side.

"Show this man to the passenger's cabin below."

"Aye, sir."

The officer held out his hand.

"Oh, yes, of course." Ephaltus removed his purse and counted fifteen gold into the officer's hand.

"This way." The boy beckoned.

Ephaltus followed him below. "How long is the voyage to Arnost?"

"About two days if the wind's with us, three if not, probably three days."

The boy showed him a small cabin with a hammock for a bed and a storage chest nailed to the floor. There was a port window and a mirror on the wall, but nothing else. It was a very sparse cabin for fifteen gold pieces.

∞

The ride across the Vestian channel to the island went by without incident, and Ephaltus arrived in Arnost safely. The forest north of Arnost was the only vegetation of any import on the island. Other than Arnost and a few scattered villages, the rest of the main island consisted of the ruins of the lost civilization of Aubria. Since almost everything had to be imported to Arnost, the cost of living there was very expensive. The main island and the smaller island surrounding it were considered some of the most beautiful places known to the six kingdoms, but most people could not afford to travel there to visit.

Arnost was old but had been partially reconstructed over the years and now was a beautiful, ancient and exotic city. Ephaltus marveled at the marble gateway from the docks to the city proper. The first thing he did was acquire lodging at the Golden Ibis Inn, which was named after the birds that live near the water on the island. The accommodations here were of the very finest money could buy. The rich from the six kingdoms paid handsomely to visit the island, so almost nothing was cheap or cheap in appearance. Once he was settled in his room, he looked over the materials he had gathered pertaining to the island and used a location spell to guide him to the ruins he needed to visit.

The first location was deep inland. It was the only forest of the islands, so he waited until first light the following day before he traveled there. The way was difficult, but surprisingly there was a well-worn path most of the way. Many visitors had hiked to the ruins as it turns out, but none knew of the place's significance. It took some fairly powerful magic, a location spell, and some scrutiny to find the doorway into the chamber where the scroll of the Cryonias was rumored to be kept. Once he was in the chamber, after using a spell to get the hidden doorway opened, he found that his magic became null. No matter how powerful a spell he tried, none would work. Somehow, magic was negated completely in this place.

"Hmm, good thing I brought a tinderbox and flint." He said to himself. He lit a torch the old fashioned way, and it disintegrated in his hands, almost burning him. It seems hundreds of years made the ancient torches brittle. He exited the chamber due to it being too dark to think of an alternative light source. He lit the top of his staff, but as soon as he entered the chamber, the magical light would go out. He scoured the surrounding area until he found a hole in the top of what he estimated must have been the chamber below. He cupped his hands and dug it around the hole until he could see inside. The chamber was well lit now. He rushed to the entrance and descended into the chamber. The light was reflecting off a large mirror into the chambers beyond. Since it was morning, he had several hours to explore before the sun moved too far west to strike the reflective mirror.

Inside the long, now well-lit room, he came to what looked like an altar. Upon the altar was a plaque with strange writing on it. Since he could not use magic, Ephaltus had no way to read the writing. It was not in any language he understood or could read. He examined around the shiny tablet for any traps or abnormalities and finding none with the naked eye, he touched it. Immediately he regretted it. The room began to spin, and he became disoriented. He closed his eyes and when he opened them again a second later, he was in a chamber surrounded by stars. The floor appeared to be glass and there was a desk ahead of him. He approached the glass desk and looked at the tablet there. The letters began to shift until they settled into something he could read. It read: Greetings to anyone who made it this far. You are seeking the lost seventh god. He does not wish to be found, nor do we wish for you to find him. Around you is an abyss. You have two choices. First you can stay here and die of starvation and thirst, or second you can jump off the platform into the abyss, never to be seen from again. Congratulations on finding the chamber of the god Cryonias. It's just too bad for you that you did. The tablet was signed Cryonias, god of the abyss.

Ephaltus tried to use magic to no avail. He could not teleport. He could not use any magic at all. He couldn't even use the stone he brought from the Arsenal of the Way to contact Marlee. He was truly trapped.

Chapter 23
Abominations

When the sun set and the rest of the light of day subsided, Thessa and Sarren left the inn to explore the city. Talt was nestled in the largest forest of the kingdom of Vestia, the resident kingdom of the king of the six kingdoms. The city had guards from the king as well as guards of their own, being that it was the capital of Vestia, but there were not nearly as many as would be in King's Cross to the east. Thessa stayed close to Sarren as she led her through the streets to the seedy north side of Talt. The northern gate was where the smugglers from Ironhold, in southern Adendalind, entered the city with their illicit goods. There were two taverns there, both filled with the kind of people Thessa was looking for according to Sarren.

If you want my instruction, I can tell you how to find those you seek.

"Yes, of course. Tell me."

Your power lies in death and the evil in men's hearts. You can sense the power in death on people. If they have killed, even if they are a soldier, you can sense it on them. It feels like a strong pull to that person. The more death surrounding them, the bigger the pull. If you open yourself up to it. You have to clear your mind and search for it with your feelings or you get nothing. She cocked her head. *Are you sure you want to look like that in the tavern?*

"Good point, but I have not made any blood feeders or caused any deaths. The magic won't work. I am stuck this way."

No, you can revert back to your normal look. Once you create a blood feeder, you can use the magic to change back.

"I don't want to change back. What if my mother finds out I was here? I had better find someone to change into a vampire before I go into the tavern."

All right, go into the alley behind one of the taverns. There is always something shockingly bad going on in the alleys.

Thessa nodded and rounded the corner to see a man who seemed to be hugging the side of the building When she got closer, she realized he had a woman pinned to the wall. He was kissing her neck. The woman saw Thessa and mouthed the words help me.

"Ah hem." Thessa said.

The man turned his head slightly to get a look at her, "Bugger off!"

"I think you should let that woman go."

He turned abruptly, "I said bugger off!" The woman slipped from his grip and hastened her way down the alley, out of sight.

"Now see what you did, I was having myself a little kiss." He stumbled closer to her. "I guess you will be the one giving me a kiss now then."

Thessa backed up and let her mind wander. She let her feelings run rampant and the man became a tremendous pull on her soul.

He had not just killed, he had done terrible things to both men and women, mostly to women. Thessa's revulsion almost made her sick. "Stay back."

"Why? You ran off my date now you must take her place." He walked toward her a little faster.

Thessa was frightened, she had never done this sort of thing on purpose. She had never given into her power as the Black Mage. "I am warning you. You don't want to come any nearer to me."

"I'll tell you what, you are one nice looking woman, I would be honored to steal a kiss from the likes of you."

Sarren was just out of sight in the darkness of the alley entrance. *Do it! Let go! Stop holding back. I am watching the street, there is no one coming.*

Thessa closed her eyes and let the flood of power she had pinned up inside flow into her. She was not prepared for the deluge of feelings that rushed into her. Her mother, the memory of being a blood feeder, the memory of all the kills she made as a blood feeder, and the anger she felt for both Sarren and Cassany. Her hands and arms felt red hot, and whisps of red mist blew up from behind her. The man stopped his pursuit in awe.

"What in the two hells are you."

She thrust the red mist over the man, and he froze in terror. Her canine teeth began to grow and curve out of her mouth and her face felt hot. She felt overwhelmed with the hunger. Streaks of red lightning flashed around her head, and she lurched forward like a ravenous cat focused on its prey. Her teeth sunk into the startled man's neck. She could feel the life leaving him and entering her. It only took seconds, and the man fell to the ground, convulsing in the throes of death. She had done it! She had used her powers of death to turn a truly evil man into her minion.

How do you feel?

"Unholy!" she said, "this is what the pleasure Cassany gifted to the Black Mage feels like?"

Yes, and now she has you, but you had no choice. You would have had to give in sooner or later.

"Where do I send this man after he turns?"

Send him into the woods to wait for further instructions. Pick a spot. You can send them all there to wait for you. You can build your army to defeat Tanyth.

When the man stopped convulsing, he stood. "Go into the woods, find a small clearing and wait for me there. Kill anyone who approaches you who is not someone I send."

"Understood mistress," he said. He walked off toward the north gate. Thessa rounded on Sarren, who was still in the shadows. She could see her there clearly now. "Who's next?"

There goes one now. Sarren pointed her paw at a young man stumbling along the side of the tavern. Thessa moved into the shadows as the man walked by them. She let her feelings go and felt the pull toward him. It must have been a good night to catch men who had done unspeakable things to women and children. Her anger filled her senses as she saw the images in her mind. She leaned down close to Sarren's furry ear, "This one is worse than the last one."

Then you know what you must do.

Thessa stalked the young man into the alleyway. He would not get away with the horrible things he had done. This man was the perfect candidate for becoming one of her blood feeders. He needed to pay, and this time he would pay with his life. She let the red mist flow behind her again. It was a blood red mist coming from seemingly thin air. She could guide it, and she sent it to ensnare the young man. He froze. Thessa was behind him, but she could feel his fear and she imagined his face twisted in terror just like the first one. She moved in to transform him and was surprised to hear him whimpering.

"Please, what are you doing?"

Thessa was terrified and angry at the same time. She didn't know they could speak to her and plead. She attacked before he could say anything else. The same convulsions the first man had gone through made this man writhe as well. When he was done, she sent him away to join the other she had created. She faced Sarren, who was still in the shadows. She could see the cat as if she were in full daylight standing in the sunlight, "You didn't tell me they could talk or plead for their lives! I can't do this if they beg me to let them go. This is more difficult than I thought. I don't know if I can do it even if they do deserve it."

Why not? They are still the evil men you sensed they were. They are undeserving of your sympathy. You must never forget that about them. Making them into blood feeders gives you power beyond anything you could have imagined without them.

"I do feel better physically than I ever have before. How will I use this power in the tournament? I can't turn people in the arena."

You try to turn the other mages. Also, the more blood feeders you make and have out in the world, the more power you will have. You can draw on them for your strength. If you have none, you are weak.

"I don't know if I can do this long enough to build an army to go after Tanyth, no matter how good it feels."

Sure you can. You just have to hate him enough and want to protect your interests enough to keep doing it. It gets easier over time.

"Are they all men or do women do bad things too?"

Women are just as guilty, don't worry.

Thessa grinned, "Then I want to turn one of them next." She started toward the tavern entrance. She suppressed the voice inside her telling her what she was doing was wrong. She was the Black Mage and this was her destiny.

You are still the pretty Zarina.

"Yes, I know. You catch more flies with honey. Why should I change?"

Well, because the power was given to you to change, no one recognizes you as some crazed vampire and hunts you down. You can still be a pretty woman.

Thessa hesitated, "Maybe you're right." She used the power and changed her appearance into a lovely young blonde woman. She looked for Sarren in the shadows, and they had gotten a bit dimmer. "A moment ago, I could see you as if you were in broad daylight, but now the surrounding darkness is dimmer."

You only created two blood feeders. If you want to keep the power, you can drain it from them or keep adding more. The more you have, the longer your power will regenerate and the more power you will retain.

"Stay out here. I doubt you would last long inside." Thessa entered the tavern. The place was loud, smoky, and smelled of old boots, ale, and unwashed bodies. She immediately stood out. All eyes seemed to turn to her. She tried to hide her nervousness behind a wide smile.

"Ay, you lost lady?" A near toothless man shouted at her from somewhere left of her.

"Yeah, you must 'ave lost yer way." Another said.

Not knowing what to do, she let the red mist flow along the floor of the full tavern. No one seemed to notice at first until it began to ensnare people.

"Hey, what is this on the floor?" A woman shouted as she tried to pull free. Others looked upon Thessa in terror. She let the mist gather quickly around the tavern. She had not intended to turn the whole place, but this was her first time and she didn't know what kind of person she needed to look like to blend into a place like this. Besides, Sarren said, the more she turned the more power she would have. She let her fangs grow, and she bared them instinctively.

"Oh, by the two hells and the gods, what are you?" The barman said from behind the counter.

"Cursed!" It was all Thessa could think of saying. She moved at lightning speed as the charged red lighting around her also struck and numbed the patrons around her as she went. She was glad to take on as many people as she wished, and she did. She let their shouts and cries fall on deaf ears as she worked her way through the tavern. A new patron entered as she did her work, and was ensnared as soon as he entered the mist. She turned on him and made him her last victim. Sarren rushed into the tavern from outside before the doors closed her out.

What did you do? Look at all this. You were supposed to be discreet. As soon as the people of this city realize a whole tavern full of people is missing, they will know what you have done!

Thessa stopped, "Let them know!"

But you can't hide from this.

"Let Cassany worry about that. She made me the way I am." The people began to awaken as blood feeders. "Go to the clearing and wait for me! Go to your brethren." The people began moving toward the door. Thessa followed to dispose of any guards or people who should show up and get in their way as they traveled through the north gate and into the forest beyond. Sarren sighed and followed after her.

Chapter 24
Life and Death

Before dawn, Thessa had created a small army from the two taverns of Talt to Sarren's utter horror. Even though the people she converted were criminals and the like, when the city wakes for the coming day and discovers what has happened, they will be livid. Sarren tried again and again to warn her, but she ignored the cat's pleas. Thessa joined her converted blood feeders in the clearing where she had sent them. She moved them through the forest for the rest of the night until the first light of day descended to the southern gates of the city of Ironhold. There, she found a suitable place to hide among some trees for the day.

Did you forget I was once the Black Mage? I know what I am talking about! Sarren said to Thessa when she was settled for the day.

"I hear what you are saying, but you're wrong. I have thought this out. These were truly bad people. The city leaders will do nothing. They will be glad to get rid of them."

You assume a lot. People don't like a lot of former criminal vampires roaming their kingdoms.

"There's nothing they can do about it. I am the Black Mage, and I am in control of the blood feeders. Nothing will happen to me until after the tournament. Cassany and the Tourney Master will see to that, and if one of the city's elders wants to hang me for cleaning out their criminals, the one whose hand does the deed will be the new Black Mage. They wouldn't dare! Even if someone did take my place, this would all start over again, only this time it may be their sons and daughters rather than their criminals. When you talk to Cassany before I do, tell her to have a talk with the civic leaders and explain it to them. This will solve a lot of their problems."

You have really lost your mind. I was not even this blatant. These were people, and the civic leaders will still condemn it.

"They are too corrupt. This is a simple solution." She cut her eyes at the cat, "You of all people are trying to tell me you have the moral ground here? You have done far worse, Sarren."

Maybe so, but that doesn't make what you are doing right.

"That's just it, isn't it? I am damned if I do and damned if I don't. I am cursed and now I am embracing that curse for better or for worse."

Sarren curled up on a soft plot of long grass near the dying camp fire, "it's for worse."

Tessa concentrated and used her death abilities to seek out Sir Danton and Tanyth's blood feeders. Sure enough, she felt them traveling north from Emlestra. She wondered if she could use her magic to move her small army to the arena to intercept him. Then she got an idea. She made sure Sarren was asleep and then she slowly moved away from her pallet bedding. It was no small feat to move away from a cat without rousing her. Once she was clear of Sarren and the others, she made a plea to Marlee.

"Marlee, I have been told you watch us sometimes through a magical lens. If you are somehow watching me now, I need to warn you there is an army of blood feeders I technically created but do not control heading for you and the arena. He intends to take you hostage in order to force your sister into making a poison. If you can hear me, take precautions. Your sister is also on the way there to help you. I am bringing my own force to thwart this other bunch of blood feeders. I don't know how this all works, but I hope you can hear me." She waited for a few minutes to see if there might be some kind of sign and then made her way back to camp.

When night fell, Thessa used her death magic and found another tavern full of undesirable people. She turned them all. She didn't try to find more. Instead, she joined the two forces together and marched toward the arena. Her senses told her that Tanyth was closing in, so she had to leave now in order to intercept him on time. She also knew that Sarren was probably right about the city civic leaders missing their citizens, but she had to hope she was right, and they would turn a blind eye to her doings in order to take credit for getting rid of the criminals. She could not afford to feel bad or guilty about it now. She had to push on because the world as she knew it was at stake. She also owed Gaelyn the chance to return to normal, even if their relationship was over before it really got started. She looked at the rising sun. "Where are you, mother?"

The way to the arena was basically due west from the city of Ironhold, and Thessa drove her force as fast as they could go, which was actually painfully slow. She was exhausted by the time the first day had ended. After they had left the forest and entered into the grasslands, the trees became few and far between so they had to stop for the night out in the open, underneath the stars. The second day was just as slow. Each night she kept looking with her magic to see how far Danton and Tanyth had gotten. Thankfully, they also moved slowly.

On the third day, her force had made a little better progress until the roots came. Large treelike roots came from underneath the ground and Thessa knew they had to be magical because there was only grass as far as she could see, with mesquite tress dotting the landscape here and there. The Green Mage had found them. When they were all halted by the roots, Thessa saw Teoni walking over a small hill ahead. She moved deliberately, and Thessa knew she planned to stop them permanently. She had no idea the real threat to her sister was moving up from the south.

"Black Mage," Teoni began, "Turn back and I will let you all go." She raised a line of roots about waste high to both sides.

Thessa used her magic and freed some of the men in the front then she moved into a position where Teoni could hear her clearly, "Get out of the way, Green Mage" She didn't wait for the reply but instead sent her freed men ahead toward Teoni's lines.

"Don't do this, Thessa. Don't take any more steps toward the arena."

"You fool! You have been listening to the wrong people. I am trying to do what is right! I am trying to stop the real force that's trying to capture your sister."

"No, I have found you with a small army moving directly west. It's you who are bringing an army of blood feeders to destroy the arena. That's all I need to know."

"Whoever told you that was sent by Cassany to deceive you. I am here to help."

"I see how you are trying to help. You have created blood feeders? When did you decide you were a killer?"

"I will not be lectured by you. You know it is a matter of life and death."

"I guess that's what we are, Thessa. I'm life and you are death." She commanded the ground roots to stop the men running toward her while keeping the larger roots near her at bay. She rooted the men running toward her to the ground again.

Chapter 25
White Mage

Fia, who was watching from a distance, decided to intervene, "This is not about to end well," she said as she made her way between the two rivals.

"What are you doing here, Fia?" Thessa asked.

"I followed you. I'm sorry, but I just couldn't leave things the way they were between us."

"You betrayed my trust and friendship with what you did, and I don't think I can get over it."

"I know and I want to make it up to you."

Teoni cleared her throat, "I think this is all a bit uncomfortable."

"Just a moment, Greeny." Fia said. "I need to make amends before we team up on you."

Teoni immediately rooted Fia to the ground.

"What are you doing? Fia asked.

"I am not waiting for you two to team up on me!"

"It was a figure of speech." She turned back to Thessa, "I sent word of where you are to your mother, your real mother; she should be on her way soon."

"Normally, that would make things worse, but this time it's actually a good thing." Thessa said. "I may not forgive you quite yet, but that is a step in the right direction."

"Now, as for you." Fia addressed Teoni, "She really is trying to help, I think. I was eavesdropping on her, and she seems to be on your side."

"I am trying to help. I promise. Your sister is in danger and not by me."

Teoni stared into Thessa's eyes for a long moment, "I want to believe you and you seem sincere, but if you betray me once I have let my guard down, I will not stop until you are both dead, even if I have to wait for the tournament to do it."

"Threats?" Fia said scathingly.

"I would do the same. I don't care if it is a threat. As long as you let us go, I'll take it."

Teoni released all Thessa's forces. The Black Mage then commanded them to move toward the arena once more. She checked to see where Tanyth was and realized he had gained some ground on them while they were delayed.

"Damn, they have gained ground. We must hurry if we are going to defend Marlee." Thessa said.

They pushed the blood feeders as hard as they could, but Sarren had been right, they were difficult to control. "We need to move faster."

Fia motioned for them to stop.

"We don't have time to stop." Thessa said. Fia was insistent, so they came to a halt.

Fia rummaged around in a bag and then produced a wooden flute.

"Good idea, we can march faster with the tempo of the music." Thessa said.

"No, this is a magical flute of speed stepping. Watch!" She winked and then began playing the flute and moving into a light jog. "Okay, command them to move. They have to be moving."

Thessa made them move and as soon as they began walking they were in a jog behind Fia.

Thessa looked at Teoni and shrugged, "Let's follow."

After an exhausting third day and a more exhausting fourth day, the arena was finally in sight. During the third night, Teoni decided to sleep elsewhere. Thessa knew it was because she was uncomfortable with two of her traditional enemies sleeping nearby. Trust, or lack of it, made her seek somewhere else to rest. Thessa would prove herself soon enough.

When they had gotten closer, Fia stood next to Thessa with the arena in sight, "I don't really know what you are doing. I was bluffing, just trying to defuse the situation. You say you are keeping us all safe but doing this? I hope you know what you're doing, my friend. I fear you may face some grave consequences if you ever go near Ironhold or Talt again." She surveyed the tall walls of the arena, "What would you have me do? I am at your service."

"It's time to end this. I am trying to save the arena and the Tourney Master. I am not sure why no one believes me."

"Um, well, you are a big 'ol bundle of death, you see."

"That reminds me. Where is Sarren?"

Fia pointed behind a couple of the blood feeders, "She's over there. Don't worry. I have been watching that treacherous snake closely the whole time. Why you allow her to travel with you and stay with you, *and* give you advice, I will never know. She is always only thinking of herself."

"Well, Cassany trusts her more than I do. I don't let her words get to me, mostly. Every once in a while I almost forget and start to trust her, but you must understand I never will trust her fully. If she didn't need me to gain her freedom, I would probably already be dead. No, Fia, I trust you more than I trust her, and you have betrayed me more than once already."

"Hey, it was one time."

Thessa just grinned and kept walking toward the arena.

"It seems quiet." Fia observed.

"Thanks to you, we are here early. I would say Tanyth is still at least a half day away." She pointed ahead to where Teoni was rushing to get to the arena. "She has time to go find her sister and warn her." Thessa sighed, "Do you have anything in your magic repertoire to find Ephaltus or to bring him back here?"

"Sadly, no. I could probably find him, but bringing him where would take a long while unless he could use a portal here. We should ask Marlee how they get around. I know they can travel pretty fast around the six kingdoms."

Thessa allowed the blood feeders to camp near the arena. She had to sacrifice a few of them in order to feed the others. It was a gruesome thing, but she remembered that's how they would do it when she was a blood feeder and there was not a good source of blood nearby.

Teoni and Marlee met Fia and Thessa at the gate. Marlee addressed Thessa, "I wanted to thank you for the warning. I did see your message that night. I have not been able to contact Ephaltus. Something has happened to him."

"Oh, I can find him." Fia said. "How do you two get around the six kingdoms, anyway?"

Marlee brightened, "He can instantly portal back here. If you have some magic to get to him, he can return."

Fia reached into her bag and pulled out a music box. "When you are all at a safe distance where you can't hear the music in the box clearly, I will go to him."

"Oh, thank you, Fia." Marlee said. "I don't think he had any clue something like this would happen when he left me here in charge."

"All right, you three run along and I will go get him." Fia said.

The rest made their way quickly to the gateway of the arena. Thessa looked back to see Fia blink out. "Who would have thought." She said, "The White Mage to the rescue."

Chapter 26
The Last Stand

Tanyth's army poured over the hill on the north side of the arena. The two Sanquinators had been busy and the army they had built was much larger than Thessa had anticipated. In fact, something had been able to hide much of the force from her senses. They were a frightening lot, much more so than her own force. They were a horde of mindless undead bent on the destruction of the arena gates and anyone who got in their way. Thessa sent her forces to intercept them, and if all goes well, they will reach them before the horde will be able to breach the arena gates or walls, which were vulnerable due to the renovations. Since the vegetation had not yet been cleared completely away from the walls, Teoni could use it to trap some of the marauders as they passed by. The arena proper was enormous, but Tanyth was not interested in conquering it. He was interested in getting to the Arsenal of the Way and the Earth Chamber, and Thessa knew it. She diverted some of her army to block Tanyth's route into the wooded area where Marlee and the dryads were housed.

"Sarren, get somewhere safe. Since you are a cat, you can hide." Sarren jumped down from a wooden table and disappeared into the wooded area near where the Earth Chamber was located. Marlee found Thessa and gave her one of the special weapons from the Arsenal of the Way. It was a long shaft with a curved blade on the end, slightly reminiscent of a scythe, but the blade was curved and not attached at a right angle. "What is this?"

"I don't know. It was in the weapons rack marked for the Black Mage. I thought maybe you knew how to use it."

"I do not. I am not even sure how I am supposed to hold it. I don't think I could even swing it."

"Maybe it's enough just to look imposing."

"What defenses does this place have?"

"The dryads told me a few things, but the Tourney Master has all the knowledge and some defenses will only work for him. He didn't expect I would have to fend off an attack. He has not gotten around to explaining how everything works around here either. At least, he hasn't explained what to do in case of a full-scale attack."

"I hope Fia can find him and get him back here in time. It was irresponsible for him to leave you like this. He should have known someone would notice his absence and try to take the place by force."

"Why would they do such a thing anyway?" Marlee asked.

"Who knows. My guess would be to end the tournament insuring the current king and his family rules forever."

The gate began to rock on its wooden hinges, and one finally popped off, making the huge door sag. Thessa's small band of blood feeders waited for the breach. They all had swords or spears or whatever was handy.

"Marlee, it's you they want. Why don't you hide in the Earth Chamber?" Thessa suggested.

"Good idea." Marlee agreed.

"What, that's it. They are after you. They don't know Teoni is here. If we show that Teoni is here, maybe that will stop the attack. There are three mages here to fend them off."

Teoni joined them behind Thessa, "I don't think that matters to them at this point. Whether I am here or not, they will not stop until they get Marlee and take the arena."

Marlee scowled at her sister, "We replaced the book you stole. I know you knew we would trade places, but still! You stabbed me!"

Teoni let her sword fall, "Marlee, you know I would make the better mage and you the better Tourney Master. I did us both a favor. If you know about the book, then you know what I had planned. It made sense."

"But how did you know to stab…"

Whatever Marlee was about to say, it got cut off by the doors crashing down and the horde rushing through. Thessa's forces rushed in and clashed with Tanyth's army.

"Marlee, get to the Earth Chamber!" Thessa told her. She ran back through the wooded area.

∽

Sarren found Tanyth at the rear of his army with Sir Danton and Gaelyn. She ran up to the dark elf and meowed.

"Ah, yes, the cat. You played your part well. Cassany is pleased. She has one last task for you before you are truly free and human again.

This battle will end with the Black Mage finally accepting her place and destroying all the undead and taking their power. She has had the ability all the while. She just doesn't realize it yet, or maybe she does and is just in denial. Regardless, Cassany still wants the poison." He reached into his armor and produced a dagger. With a prick of this enchanted dagger, you shall be returned to being a human. He poked the cat with the dagger and Sarren reformed into her human form. "Take this dagger." Sarren took the dagger. "You know what you need to do?"

"Yes, I believe I do."

"Careful, don't get killed in the heat of the battle trying to find your way back into the arena walls." He grinned unnaturally. "Go on, you can do it. You can make the poison for Cassany."

"I will be careful." Sarren said, then she turned and ran excitedly toward the gates.

Tanyth stared into Gaelyn's eyes. "It's your turn to do your part, friend." Gaelyn nodded. "Go to her now." Gaelyn bounded off for the gate toward Thessa.

∾

Thessa's forces were keeping the horde at bay, but it was too easy. It seemed like Tanyth's blood feeders were weaker than hers and almost let hers kill them. Either Thessa's criminal element was paying off, or Tanyth's army was letting Thessa win. Something was not right. She glanced at Teoni, who was nearby wrapping members of the horde in strong vines and rooting others to the ground. She was able to keep the stranglers from getting away from the group and running toward the Earth Chamber. "Teoni, this is too easy. They should be overwhelming us. Why are they holding back?"

"I don't know. I didn't realize they were."

"They have superior numbers. They should be getting through. I am not even casting any spells." She watched the line of bodies as they cut through the invaders. Then she saw him. Gaelyn was getting through. Teoni rooted him. "No, let that one through. I know him."

"I am not letting him in. He's a blood feeder."

"Fine, I will go to him." Thessa climbed down the earthen work and ran to him. His eyes were pleading. All she wanted to do was get him out of the fight and somewhere where she could lock him up safely. At least long enough for her mother to get there and cure him. She took his hand and immediately with the other hand, he stabbed Thessa with a dagger. She stepped back. He could not pursue her to stab her again since he was still rooted. He swung savagely trying to get at her, but he could not move his feet. Thessa was in a total state of shock. She put her hand over her wound and fell to her backside, all the while Gaelyn was still trying to stab her. In shock, she almost didn't believe her eyes when she saw Sarren, now human once again, run past her. She watched as the woman made a direct line for Teoni. Since Sarren didn't look like a blood feeder, Teoni didn't root her right away. Thessa realized what Sarren was planning and broke a couple of men off the line to go after her. Teoni was too far away for her to yell a warning. Thessa had separated from her to go after Gaelyn. It only took a second for Sarren to surprise Teoni and plunge the dagger into the Green Mage's heart, possibly believing she would take on the mantle of the Green Mage, but she was not truly alive, Thessa had resurrected her. Tanyth grinned in triumph as he entered the gates. She had played into his hands. Teoni went down and Sarren went with her. The green mist of the Green Mage left Teoni and entered Sarren. The woman stood and shouted in glee. She had done it. She was a mage again. She turned toward Thessa and wrinkled her nose in anger. She sprinted to where Thessa lay bleeding. As Teoni's life force left her, the horde began to unroot and run into the arena. Thessa shook her head when Sarren reached her, "Sarren, the Green Mage is life and you have always been death. You have killed my friend for nothing. You are not like me. My mother cured me. I still smell the taint of death upon you. You are incompatible with the Green Mage."

"And you are compatible with the Black Mage? Look at you. You're lying there bleeding to death, and you don't have a clue as to what you need to do next."

"Give up. It won't work. The essence of the Green Mage will not stay with your black soul."

Sarren scoffed, "No, I will defeat you now. I have much more experience."

"What you have done is not the way. You are not wholly among the living. You can't kill a mage."

Sarren bent down to cut the vines from Gaelyn, "I will finally have my revenge!"

Now, Teoni's rooting spells and vines gave way. The horde began to advance. Gaelyn wriggled to get loose. If he managed it, he would grab and stab her again. Thessa braced for the worst and then, abruptly, Sarren stopped. Green goo began to pour out of her mouth. "I told you. You are not whole; you cannot be the Green Mage."

"But Tanyth told me…" She looked frantically for the elf.

"He lied." Thessa said as Sarren deteriorated with a scream into a bubbling green goo.

Gaelyn broke free and Thessa caught the hand with the dagger and tried desperately to hold him off, but her injury was making it difficult, "My mother is coming. I can have her cure you!"

"I don't care. You must die." Gaelyn said in a terrible, angry voice.

"I was once one of you. She cured me. She can cure you too."

"Die, die, DIE!"

She realized in that moment that Hana would not be able to undo what was done, at least not the way she was able to bring her back. Thessa closed her eyes, releasing the tears that were waiting to fall. She remembered how she took back the power from the blood feeder before and she willed it to happen again. She realized at that moment that she could take them all back. She was responsible for all of them, and she could unmake them all. She leaned into Gaelyn's ear. "I would have liked to have had the chance to love you." She whispered. He was the first to go. His whole being disintegrated, and the power surged through her, healing her stab wound. She stood and focused on all the blood feeders, Tanyth's and her own. She raised her arms, and they all began to go one by one, causing the dark power of death to surge into her.

Chapter 27
Futility

The first thing Thessa did when all the blood feeders were gone was to go to Teoni. Maybe she could resurrect her. She focused her power and let it flow into Teoni but nothing happened.

"You cannot resurrect her. It's too late." It was one of the dryads.

"I have done it before! I am full of power I can do it!"

"No, you are in the arena. That power does not work here."

"I will drag her out of the arena."

"It matters not. She died here in the arena. You cannot resurrect her."

"But who will be the Green Mage?"

"That is already done. The Green Mage has been made anew somewhere in the six kingdoms. Ephaltus and Marlee will have to find the new Green Mage. That's their job and it's now in their hands. Come, Marlee needs you. Take my hand and I will take you to her."

"I didn't know you could talk." Thessa said as she reached for her tiny hand.

"Of course we can if we have something worth saying."

"What about Teoni?"

"My kin will take her, do not worry." There was a rush like a sudden wind, and Thessa found herself in a kitchen. "This is the kitchen of the Earth Chamber. Marlee is through that door." She pointed the way.

Thessa stumbled slightly from being ported into the Earth Chamber but righted herself long enough to go through the door into the living quarters of the Tourney Master where Marlee saw her.

"What has happened?" She asked.

Thessa opted not to tell her about Teoni yet, "The blood feeders are all gone. I got rid of them with my dark power. I'm sorry, I must have dropped the weapon you gave me out there."

"You got rid of them?"

"Yes, I took their power. Ultimately, I created all of them and I released them. But we are not safe yet. Tanyth and Danton are still out there. I thought I got rid of all of them, but I do still feel Danton. He must have been protected by Cassany."

"Where is Teoni?" Thessa froze. "Thessa?"

"She didn't make it."

"What? Where is she?"

"The dryads are taking care of her. I didn't just leave her out there."

Marlee burst out in anger, "Why didn't you resurrect her?"

"I tried. My resurrection ability does not work in the arena on mages."

Marlee broke down. Thessa picked Marlee's head up, "Now's not the time. We will mourn later. Right now, Tanyth is out there, and he is going to try to assassinate you. He was here to assassinate all of us. The premise for him coming here was all a ruse to deceive us. I think Cassany is trying to reset the tournament as I guessed before by getting rid of you and every mage she can, even me. If Fia would have stayed, she would probably be a target as well. The five years might start over, especially if you fall.

"Oh, the other gods will be incensed!"

There came a rhythmic and systematic knocking on the tree door. Tanyth was trying to find the entrance to the Earth Chamber. Thessa moved to block the doorway, "Do you have any magic to stop him?"

"I do not have the magic of Ephaltus quite yet. He has not trained me with it much, but I do know some of it." Marlee replied. "What I have read about."

"Use it. Anything you know would be helpful. I am going to go back out there and see if I can stop him."

"Thessa, Tanyth is crafty. He is an assassin."

Thessa nodded, waited for Tanyth to move on, and then she left the defense of the Earth Chamber to Marlee and the dryads.

Once out in the forest she could see Sir Danton clearly, but he did not see her yet. She concentrated her power on him, probably drawing too much of it considering the amount of blood feeder power she had absorbed, but she didn't want him to survive. It was time for the Sanquinator, Sir Danton, to end. She drew his power, and he screamed in pain and terror as he imploded, something she didn't know she could do until just then. His carcass shriveled up and then disintegrated like the rest of the blood feeders. The power surge was immense, and she struggled to contain it. Feeling the power from the Sanquinator made her realize this was the first time she had felt it. The other Sanquinator was still out there somewhere.

"Ah, there you are, Thessa. You have done well. You have fallen into every one of my traps, but you tried so hard."

"That's far enough, dark elf. It's time to bring all this to an end. I have more than enough power to destroy you."

Tanyth dropped the sword he was carrying and also dropped his arms to his sides, "Alright, Black Mage. Here I am and I am unarmed. Destroy me"

"Not very wise considering how much power from death I have drawn into myself within the last hour." Thessa said.

"Such confidence, I love it. Do your worst."

Thessa let the power of death flow through her and she unleashed it on Tanyth. He gasped and flew backward, smashing through one of the trees behind him. Thessa smiled to herself with satisfaction until she saw him rise from where he landed. She didn't give him time to recuperate. She ran at him as fast as she could. She would turn him into a blood feeder and then she could take his power. He tried to push her away when she came toward him, but she was too fast. The red mist formed around him, and she sunk her fangs deep into his neck. The taste was all wrong, and he flung her off him to the ground. Her tongue burned, and she began to spit out the weird tasting blood. "What are you?"

"I will tell you what I tell everyone. I am something else. It is futile for the likes of you to destroy me. If I need to tear down each and every tree in this forest, so be it."

Thessa watched in horror as his face began to elongate and his body tore through his leather clothing. His eyes bulged and great wings began to grow from his back. His skin became green scales and his hair turned to reptilian ridges. He grew larger and larger until he towered above the trees. He roared with viciousness. Thessa knew at that point she was far out of her league. Tanyth Veridian was a dragon!

He demolished the trees closest to him. Thessa heard the flapping of wings and at first, she thought Tanyth must have been doing it, but a few seconds later another dragon about the size of a horse appeared and began breathing dragon fire on him. He roared in pain, and then immediately chased after the smaller dragon. Thessa took the time to run back to the Earth Chamber. She beat on the outside of the tree door, "It's me. Let me in!"

The door opened, and she rushed in, shutting it behind her, "Tanyth is a dragon!"

Marlee gasped, "What? We don't have a chance then."

"Where can we go? Another, smaller dragon has him occupied at the moment.

"The dryads can take us back to the arena through a portal." Marlee said. "Maybe we can escape from there.

"Good, come on, we have to leave. He's going to tear down every tree until he crushes the Earth Chamber."

They went into the kitchen and the dryads took them to the arena. Tanyth was still chasing after the smaller dragon and knocking down walls of the arena in the process. "This isn't good enough. We have to find somewhere to hide." Thessa said.

"The Arsenal of the Way?" Marlee suggested.

"Can we make it? I think this is it." Thessa said.

"I think we can. We have to try. I have an idea. You sent Fia after Ephaltus. I can use the Ocularius Magnus to find Fia and see where they are."

"Lead the way!" Thessa said, "We'll just have to risk it."

Marlee led them to the Arsenal while Tanyth kept trying to return to the forest. The smaller dragon's fire was the only thing that seemed to hurt him.

In the arsenal, they rushed to the Ocularius and Marlee began turning knobs, "Ephaltus will kill me for not calibrating it first, but this is an emergency." The lens roared to life, and she turned a color-coded knob to the color white. The lens focused on a room with stars for walls and a glass floor. Fia and Ephaltus were arguing about something. "There they are." Marlee said.

"Where in the two hells are they?" Thessa asked.

"The Ocularius says the Sunken Islands."

"Use the Ocularius portal," One of the attending dryads said. "The Ocularius works both ways. Its sees all and can bring them to you."

Marlee looked stunned, "I didn't know you could talk."

The dryad looked annoyed, "Use that lever there and point that smaller lens at that platform." She pointed to a smaller platform just to the left of the machine.

"I wondered what that was for." She did as the dryad said and pulled another lever, which the dyad pointed out above the first one. There was a blinding flash of light and a whoosh of air as the Ocularius began spinning wildly. Another flash of light and Ephaltus and Fia were both lying on the platform unconscious.

Chapter 28
The Bramble Path

Thessa rushed to the platform where Ephaltus was the first to awaken. He pushed himself up from the platform with Thessa's help. Fia began to stir.

Ephaltus looked at the Ocularius Magnus as it spun down. "I never thought I would say this but bless this infernal machine!" There came a rumbling from outside the Arsenal. "What in the two hells is going on here?"

Marlee came down from the machine, "We are under attack."

"By whom?" He looked around at Thessa and the dryads. "What has happened? Marlee?"

"There is a dragon named Tanyth Veridian outside."

"The assassin? Who sent him here?"

Thessa spoke up, "I believe it was Cassany."

"Of course it was." Ephaltus lamented.

"Shelayla is keeping him busy." Marlee said.

Ephaltus spun around to look at her, "You know who Shelayla is?"

"Yes, she is part of the history of the Tourney Masters."

"Yes, you are correct. My mind is a little befuddled by the portal." He exited the Ocularius Room into the Arsenal. He popped his head back in for a brief moment, "Well, are you coming Marlee? This is something you should know."

Marlee followed him with Thessa and Fia close behind.

Fia put her hand on Thessa's shoulder, "I think I'm going to be sick."

"Don't get sick on me." Thessa said.

Ephaltus led them into a room set aside from the rest. "When there is a threat to the arena of this scale, the gods have provided us with this." He reached for a small box about the size of an apple. "It's something Cassany knows about and why she has been spying on me to see when I'm gone. I should have shown it to you earlier, but I had no idea she was going to try something like this." He led them out of the Arsenal to the arena. The place had been wrecked, first by the blood feeders and now by the dragons. "Good gods, they have destroyed the place. The other gods are going to throw a fit."

"What are you going to do? Kill the dragon?"

"That's not really what I do. Most of the gods don't like us killing their creations." He took the box and set it on the ground. "Bring him over here, Shelayla." He shouted.

The smaller dragon brought Tanyth to the arena where he landed. Shelayla flew off.

"Well, you are all here now. I'll deal with that little flying menace shortly. First, I will complete the job I came here for!" He breathed in and smoke began to come from his nostrils. Ephaltus whispered a few magic words and punted the box at the dragon as he was breathing fire. A great shield erupted from the box and covered the dragon completely, then it began to shrink rapidly and return to the box, dragon and all. Ephaltus walked to the box and picked it up. "I will give him to the gods to decide his fate. We will have to meet with them, and I suppose I will have to explain where I was all this time." He looked around the arena, "What a mess I have made of things." He put the box in his pocket, "You had all better come to the Earth Chamber and have supper. I need to hear the whole story of what happened here, and I am starving. Plus, we need to hurry and eat. I get the feeling I am going to be called to a lot of meetings in the very near future."

"The gods knew there might be a dragon? That's what the box was for?"

"What...no, the box adapts to the situation."

"Ah, okay."

"Tell the dryads I could use some water too. I was trapped for quite some time."

༄

The seventh god, Cryonias, turned from his looking glass, "So, he is a Tourney Master. Clever, very clever. No one has ever escaped my trap in all the years of my exile."

"Well, he did have help. He didn't figure it out himself."

"Clydus, you silly dragon! Does that matter, my friend?"

"I guess not," the small red dragon, about the size of a horse, said as he perched on the enormous shoulder of the seventh god.

"I will have to send this, Ephaltus, a few more clues. Which one would you prefer, Clydus?"

"Oh, the Bramble Path. Make him follow the Bramble Path."

Cryonias chuckled, "All right, the Bramble Path it is."

༄

Lylah jolted out of bed and ran to the window to look at the garden. A strange green mist dissipated into the air around her, but she didn't stop to investigate it. She was more worried the storm from the previous night and its large hailstones might have destroyed the plants. When she gazed out the window, her worst fears had come true. She rushed into the living quarters of the royal gardener, her father, and noticed her mother crying on his shoulder.

"We will be ruined, Den. The king will punish you and take away our food privileges."

"It will be all right, dear. I will just explain to him what happened. We cannot be blamed for the acts of the gods." Lylah opened the door and her parents both looked at her. She saw the horror in their faces and then she bolted out the front door.

"It's no use. They are not salvageable." Her father called after her. Still, Layla went out to the plants. She walked through the garden until she came to her favorite plants, the foxgloves. She reached down to touch one of them and to her surprise the heart-healing plant's stems reached up to her. She could feel the plant's pain when it touched her. She could have sworn the plant whispered to her for help. Overwhelmed, she dropped to her knees and wished, no willed, for the plants to be healed. She couldn't bear the cries of them as they called to her for help. She instinctively thrust her hands into the soil and released her will. A green tinge covered the gardens, and the plants began to recover before her eyes. She pulled her hands from the soil and examined them. They shimmered with a green aura. She gasped as the memories came. They were forced into her mind until she felt her eyes would burst from her head. They were memories, knowledge, and thoughts from someone else, someone who once called herself the Green Mage. Lylah's parents ran out into the garden of now healthy plants to check on their daughter, who had just fainted.

End of *Black Mage Cursed*
Green Mage Metamorphosis is the next book in the Tournament of Mages series
The Direct URL to sign up to be notified of new releases is: shorturl.at/kntL7
Visit my website: www.cleavebourbon.com
Visit my You Tube Channel: shorturl.at/uDFTZ

Tournament of Mages Series:
Red Mage: Ascending Book 1
Blue Mage: Equinox Book 2
Black Mage: Cursed Book 3
Green Mage: Metamorphosis Book 4
Grey Mage: Protector Book 5
White Mage: Rhapsody Book 6
Enter the Arena Book 7
Prequel The Seventh God

Shadows of the First Trine Series:
Book 1 The Harrowing Path
Book 2 Serpent in the Mist
Book 3 Seer of Shadows
Book 4 Undead Inheritance
Book 5 Fury of the Lich
Prequel Shadows of Yesterday

War of the Oracle Series:
Dragon's Blood Book 1
The Cursed Phylactery Book 2
Wizards of War Book 3
Lurker in the Shadows Book 4

Adendalind – An eastern elvish kingdom with mountains and forests. It is believed to be the oldest kingdom.

Ag Caderan – The southern kingdom of men and elves. The southernmost section of the Asir desert ends in the north of this kingdom, giving way to an arid steppe climate. The western section of this kingdom, west of the Asa River, is wet and rainy.

Andiel – The god patron of the Red Mage.

Asrion – The patron god of the Grey Mage

The Arena of the Six Kingdoms – The complex used in the Tournament of Mages. It is a complex field that can morph into just about anything the Tourney Master can think of. It's the testing grounds for the six mages.

Arran – The current Blue Mage

Arsenal of the Way – Arsenal located in the arena complex. It's where all the equipment for the tournament is kept. It also houses the six orbs, magical portals that allow the Tourney Master to instantly travel to any of the mages.

Asirad – Mostly desert kingdom of nomadic men. Sixty percent of the kingdom is a deadly desert.

Asleth – The current Grey Mage, born in Adendalind, and ally to Hana. He is older and better trained than Hana, so he becomes invaluable to her.

Benera – Patron god of the Blue Mage.

Blood Feeder/Vampyre – A creation of the Black Mage's power. They are former men or elves bitten by the master Vampyre, who was directly created by the Black Mage or might be the Black Mage. They are part of the Black Mage's dominion over death and the dead.

Craessa – Southernmost kingdom of elves and a few high men. Craessa is a forested kingdom with lush southern grasslands.

Cryonias – The seventh god. He is the god of the arcane (ancient) magic. He was exiled and imprisoned by the other gods.

The Earth Chamber – The home of the Tourney Master, kept and maintained by woodland nymphs called dryads. The dryads take care of the grounds while the Tourney Master is sleeping, and they take care of the Tourney Master's needs when he/she is awake.

Ephaltus – The eighty-seventh Tourney Master of the Tournament of Mages. He is a wizard immune to all the magic of the six mages. He awakens five years before the tournament is to take place each century to prepare and aid the six mages as they train.

Fia – The current White Mage.

Gaelyn – Suitor of Thessa in the marketplace of Emlestra, Craessa.

Gwade – Former Red Mage from the last Tournament of Mages. He is well over one hundred years old. He forfeited the title of rule to the first runner-up.

Hana/Ilhana – The Red Mage, handmaiden for the Sephera family. Little is known about her at this writing.

Helious – The patron god of the White Mage.

Magi – currency used in Craessa. It comes in copper magi, silver magi, and gold magi. It's call magi because it is produced magically and magically sealed to protect against counterfeiting.

Marlee – The eighty-eighth Tourney Master and current apprentice to Ephaltus, who is scheduled to retire. She is the sister of Teoni.

Nateria – The patron god of the Green Mage.

Ocularius Magnus – Giant lens mounted at the top of the Arsenal of the Way. It allows the Tourney Master to watch and look in on all six mages. It can be corrupted by the gods, so the Tourney Master can't be sure that what he or she is seeing is what is really happening unless they magically calibrate it before each use.

Sarren/ Lord Sarren – Antagonist of Hana. Later Thessa, as the Black Mage, forcers Sarren to serve her in the guise of a house cat.

The Sepheras – Family Hana works for. Moira, the mother. Lord Immoran, the father. Gwendrel, the eldest daughter. Thaxa, the middle child. Terad, the youngest.

Shelayla – Dragon not bigger than a horse who guards Ephaltus' treasures in his hidden vault.

Talt – Capital city of Vestia. Although it is the capital, it is relatively small for a city.

Tamania – Northernmost kingdom dominated mostly by men. Tamania is also home to several nomadic tribes that move back and forth through the plains and deserts of both Tamania and Asirad. It is the most mountainous of all six kingdoms.

Teoni/Thelee – Sister to Marlee, she is the Green Mage. She took the mantle of Green Mage by locating and killing the true-born Green Mage. Thelee is her elvish name. She was born in Craessa.

Tharen – Distant nephew of Gwade. He takes care of the old Red Mage at a cottage in Adendalind.

The Suckling Pig – An inn located in the city of Emlestra

Tournament of Mages – Tired of seeing their beloved people constantly war and kill each other, the gods of the six kingdoms formed the Tournament of Mages. One mage capable of leading would be born in each kingdom every one hundred years. They come to the arena to compete in both mental and physical feats to determine who will lead the six kingdoms for the next century. The tournament is overseen by the Tourney Master.

Tourney Master – A wizard immune to all the mages' various magic. It is his job to maintain the arena complex and help the mages. It is also his job to keep cheating to a minimum.

The Two Hells – In the religion of the six kingdoms, there are two hells. The first hell is relatively mild and is for those who may have a chance to redeem themselves. The second hell or lower hell is for the worst of the worst. They will never redeem themselves and will be tormented forever. Saying or using "hells" or "two hells" or using a phrase such as "What in the two hells is that!" is common in all six kingdoms.

Vestia – Eastern kingdom mostly comprised of men and high men. The northern part of the kingdom is forest, and the lower part is lush grassland.

Warden – A sheriff or type of policeman of the six kingdoms. They differ from kingdom to kingdom.

Zedy – Former White Mage and current watcher/reviewer of the Blue Mage.

www.ingramcontent.com/pod-product-compliance
Lightning Source LLC
LaVergne TN
LVHW091544060526
838200LV00036B/698